Homerun Daddy
Timberwood Cove: Book 1

Liam Kingsley
© 2019
Disclaimer

Contents

Chapter 1 - Jaxon

I pulled up in front of the imposing façade of Wolf Lodge and cut the engine of my car. What could my father need to talk about that had prompted him to schedule an actual appointment with him here at his office?

To everyone else, Greer Parsons was alpha leader of the Timberwood Cove Wolf Pack. To me, he was just Dad. While I came to the lodge for any official shifter business, typically Dad talked to me about things in a more relaxed setting. Which meant that whatever this meeting was about, it was a big deal if we were meeting at the pack's headquarters.

I climbed from my car and drew in a deep, steadying breath, pushing away any uncertainty and donning the steel exterior I put on for the world. Whatever it was, I was up to the task.

The crisp spring air and scent of pine from the surrounding forest filled my lungs. The sun was shining today, something that was more than welcome after the gray Pacific Northwest winter that was still hanging on. Today, though, felt like spring was finally arriving.

Walking up the steps to the lodge, I nodded hello to a few of the elder shifters who were sitting on the wraparound porch of the large wooden cabin. Cabin didn't really fit as an accurate picture of the massive lodge, since it was more like a mansion, but it still managed to have a cozy, welcoming vibe.

I stepped into the foyer and looked around. There weren't many shifters around at ten o'clock in the morning as most of them were at work or off doing errands so I headed directly to my father's office and rapped on the door.

"Hey, Dad," I said, stepping inside without waiting for an answer.

Greer gave me a welcoming smile from where he was sitting behind a massive mahogany desk, his phone pressed to his ear. He gestured for me to have a seat in one of the two brown leather chairs in front of his desk.

This really was some official shit if we were meeting with the desk between us. Instead of sitting down, I gave him a little privacy to finish his call and wandered over to the couches in the sitting area to one side of the office. Several panes of glass made up the entire back wall of my father's office and gave a view of the dense forest that spread out behind the lodge, the peaks of the mountains rising in the distance. They were still covered with snow, even though things had all melted down in Timberwood Cove.

I shoved my hands in my pockets, wondering again about why my father had called me here today. Over the past few years, he'd given me more of a leadership role in the pack. I supposed he could have something he wanted me to help him out with. But still, this felt awfully official.

When Dad ended the call, I turned to him as he was rising from his wingback leather desk chair.

"Jaxon," he said warmly, coming over and enveloping me in a hug. These days, I was bigger than my father, but he'd always have that commanding aura about him. The one that made the rest of the pack look up to him. Kind and fair, but firm when necessary, he was the perfect leader. And father.

"Hey, Dad," I said again, returning the hug. "How's your day been?"

"Much better now you're here." He pulled back and gave me a once over. "How about you? Keeping busy?"

I laughed. "Always."

I'd retired from professional baseball a few years back but kept busy with plenty of things. I had my investments that I watched over as well as coaching Timberwood Cove's Little League team.

"In fact, we have our new season's first practice this afternoon," I told him. I'd spent the better part of the last couple weeks preparing for it.

"Good, good." He clapped me on the back and then gestured to the desk again. "Have a seat, son."

I moved to one of the chairs, and he took the one next to it. At least we didn't have the desk between us.

"I have something important to talk to you about today, Jaxon," he said, his voice growing serious.

"I can tell. Official pack business?"

He nodded. "Very much so."

Now my curiosity was piqued even more. I leaned forward, bracing my elbows on my knees. "What's up?"

He squared his shoulders, then smiled as he trained his eyes on mine. "I'm retiring."

I sat back, blowing out a breath. That wasn't what I'd expected. At all. But he threw me for an even bigger loop with his next words.

"I'll be an elder then, son. And I want you to take over my role as pack leader."

I blinked a few times, trying to process how three sentences could totally change my world.

"What?" I finally managed to ask, hoping I didn't sound as off-kilter as I felt. I prided myself on always seeming cool, calm and collected. My steel façade. Always in control and able to handle any situation. Right now, however, I felt anything but.

My dad laughed. "Don't act so surprised. You had to know this was coming at some point."

I mean, I guessed I'd considered the possibility. It wasn't uncommon for the pack leader's alpha son to take over when he stepped down, but that was just the thing. I wasn't his biological son. He'd adopted me when I was just a young pup, and while I'd never felt like I wasn't his son in every way that mattered, I couldn't help but feel this was the one area where there was a difference.

As if he read my mind, my father said, "I don't want to hear anything about you not being the right choice. You're the obvious choice, Jaxon, for a number of reasons. Even if you weren't my son, you'd be a prime candidate. Don't sell yourself short."

He knew me better than anyone else, so of course he saw straight through my hesitations.

"It's not just that, Dad." I raked a hand through my hair and blew out a heavy breath.

He frowned. "It's not just me that agrees you'd be the perfect leader. The entire elder council thinks so."

I felt a rush of pride at his words. I'd always worked hard to prove myself in every way. Maybe even overcompensated for the fact that I was adopted—even though my dad had never made me feel any less his son, but that pride wasn't enough to quell my doubts.

I shook my head. "I don't think I'm ready," I said, hedging.

Now my father leaned back, his eyes narrowing. "I'd have to disagree. Your entire life has led up to this. Don't tell me you think I haven't prepared you well?" There was a hint of teasing in his tone, but also a bit of disappointment. Like he'd expected an entirely different reaction from me.

That made my stomach clench. I hated disappointing anyone. I went above and beyond to make sure I didn't. Now here I was disappointing the one man I wanted to please most.

"No, no, it's not that," I said quickly. "I just…"

How was I supposed to tell my father—the most important alpha among the Timberwood Cove Pack—that I didn't feel good enough to fill his shoes?

I'd spent my entire life trying to convince people I was. Apparently I'd done such a good job my father didn't seem to doubt my abilities, but it took the strongest of alphas to lead a wolf shifter pack. I meant what I said—I wasn't sure I was ready for that.

I finally settled on revealing one of my main concerns. "I haven't even found a mate, Dad. How can I be the leader of the pack when I can't guarantee I can carry on the family name?"

He laughed. "You really think that matters to me? Keeping the leadership in the family? Let me be honest with you, Jaxon. If I didn't think you were suited for the role, I'd choose someone else as my successor, son or not. You'll be a good leader simply because of who you are. If you don't have children, you'll choose someone who you see fit to pass the role onto when that time comes."

Warmth spread through my chest at his belief in me. He truly did think I was capable. That should be enough. On top of that, the elder council apparently supported his decision, but I still wasn't sure.

I really felt finding a mate was prime importance. I wanted to find someone to share my life with, to have children with. To follow in my father's footsteps. However, I was already thirty years old. Shifters much younger than me had already found their mates. It was possible I might never find mine, and without a mate… Honestly, what kind of leader could I be?

Dad leaned forward and steepled his fingers. "Look, I'm not asking for an answer today, but please know there is no one else I feel is as well-suited to the job than you. Take some time to think about it, and we'll talk more. Just know I believe in you."

It was exactly what I needed to hear. I smiled. "Thank you. And yes, I can do that."

My father visibly relaxed, then stood and reached for me, pulling me into another bear hug. "Good. I won't keep you. I know you have a lot to do, and I have plenty to keep me busy as well. We'll talk later."

"Yes, for sure," I replied, returning his hug. I wasn't sure more time to think about it would make a difference, though. I'd spent too many years doubting myself to stop now, but like I said, I was good at putting on a strong front. I smiled at my father as we said our goodbyes. Unfortunately I didn't feel any relief at seeing the disappointment retreat from his face, not when knowing that in the long run he'd only be even more disappointed when I proved I wasn't up to the job of being pack leader.

***

I threw a few more bottles of water and some electrolyte drinks into my cooler. I'd spent the last few hours since I returned home trying to focus on preparing for practice, but I hadn't been able to stop thinking about my conversation with my father.

I tried to drown out my thoughts by turning on a baseball game, but that had only seemed to amplify my anxiety. It didn't happen often these days, but I'd found myself replaying that last fateful game in my head over and over through the afternoon.

Sighing, I went to grab a protein bar to eat before practice. Images of that game flitted through my mind as I ate. How the Takoma Timberwolves had been depending on me. It was the bottom of the ninth and bases were loaded. The final game in the playoffs that would send our team to the World Series, and I was up to bat.

I cringed as I remembered the ball flying toward me, how I'd thrown everything I had into coming through for everyone. Into being the hero. Only I'd mistimed my swing, my wolf reflexes for once failing me. Instead of hitting the ball clear to the other side of the field, I'd given it a glancing blow, making an easy catch for the pitcher. The humiliation of knowing I'd lost everything we'd worked so hard for all season in one life-altering swing still plagued me now. We'd lost the game. The chance at the championship. And I'd been benched. Permanently.

I'd failed everyone. Myself most of all.

I didn't have what it takes to stay on top of my profession, so how the hell was I supposed to lead a pack and not fail them too when I'd buckled under the pressure of that game?

Frustration mingled with grief, and I forced myself back to the present. To what I had to think about now. There was a whole group of kids waiting for me to come through for them. I may have failed my team before, but I'd be damned if I failed these kids.

It had been therapeutic, coaching a team. Giving them all I had. I'd been able to take my passion for the game and throw it all into these kids. It helped me forget some of my failings. Because in spite of my history with baseball, I was a damn good coach. Being a role model gave me purpose. Helped me feel whole again in those moments when I was absorbed in teaching them the game I loved so much.

An alarm went off on my phone, and I grabbed the cooler and headed for the car. I'd already loaded it up with equipment, and Linc would have the rest for our team. Linc Travers was my best friend and my assistant coach for the Little League team.

When I pulled up at the sports complex, Linc was already there, his eight-year-old son Cole in tow. They were unloading gear from Linc's car.

"Jaxon!" Cole said, bouncing up and down as I climbed from my car. "I never thought you'd get here."

I laughed and ruffled his hair. "Right on time, buddy."

Linc grinned at me and handed me a bag of baseballs. "He's been asking how long until practice every fifteen minutes all day." He pulled a face, crossing his eyes and sticking out his tongue. "You have no idea."

Cole looked up at me, his eyes shining. "I've been working extra hard playing catch with Dad. Just wait until you see."

"Can't wait," I said, handing the baseballs off to him. "Why don't you carry these over to the field?"

He darted off, and I went to my trunk to grab my portable file bin that had all the papers of info the parents would need for the season. When I turned around, Linc was looking at me funny.

"So, when were you going to tell me?" Linc asked.

I knew Linc too well not to know what he was talking about, but how he already knew about the talk I had with my dad I had no idea. I sighed, setting the files back down.

"I haven't said yes."

Linc's eyebrows flew up and his eyes widened. "Why not? It's an amazing opportunity, Jax." When I didn't reply, he tilted his head. "Isn't it?"

I really didn't want to get into my doubts with Linc, so I shrugged. "It's just a lot of responsibility," I offered as an excuse for my hesitation.

"I get that, but there's no one who could handle it better than you."

He sounded a lot like my father had. It should have made me feel better that they believed so strongly in me. Instead, it only made me worry all the more about letting them down by not living up to their expectations.

"Hey," he added with a smirk. "If you don't want it, I'll volunteer as your replacement."

Linc would make a great leader, and he was second in line for pack alpha, if we followed the old traditions. He was sure and steady. Someone who'd never let his pack down.

Before I could say so, Cole came running back up. "Hey, can we go to dinner at Kay's after practice?"

It had become a bit of a tradition last season to hit up Kay's Diner after practices.

"Sure, I don't see why not," I said, smiling down at the eager boy, who beamed back at me. "If your dad says okay."

"Um, yeah!" Linc said with a grin.

After that, I stayed too busy to even think about the whole pack leader problem. Parents started arriving, kids ran around, laughing and joking, and we had a hell of a lot to take care of.

I headed up the introductory meeting, with Linc helping out here and there. After we'd gone over all the necessary information and fees and collected paperwork, we dove straight into practice.

It felt good to be out here, and it was a perfect afternoon. The weather had cooperated all day. The first practice of the season was always exhilarating. The excitement and energy pulsing through the air. It was a welcome distraction from my crazy day.

As practice ended, and everyone was collecting their equipment, Linc strolled over to me. "So, I meant what I said earlier. If you change your mind about being the pack—"

I cleared my throat as a parent approached with a few questions. We'd have to talk about this another time when there weren't dozens of humans in earshot. I was suddenly glad we were taking Cole to dinner. Linc wouldn't have the opportunity to question me about it anymore. Maybe by the time we did get a chance to talk, I'd have figured out my shit when it came to my father's proposition.

We finished with the parent's questions, loaded up the cars, then headed to Kay's.

"Practice was amazing!" Cole said when we grabbed a booth along the wall of Kay's. If he'd said it once, he said it a hundred times.

"I'm so glad you had fun," I said with a laugh. I was starting to see what Linc meant earlier when he'd talked about Cole going on and on about practice.

He nodded enthusiastically, practically bouncing in the booth. A server came and got our orders, then Cole went into detail about every single moment of practice.

"I think we've got a pretty good team put together this year, don't you think?" Linc asked.

"The best," I agreed.

Cole licked his lips and turned to me, then bit his lip nervously. "Coach Jaxon?"

I lifted my eyebrows at his sudden serious tone. "What's up, buddy?"

"I have this friend... He loves baseball. So much. And I'd really love if he could be on our team. I know he's late signing up, and we already have the teams formed but—" He gave me a pleading look. "But if you could still let him on, that would be amazing."

I started to tell him I wasn't sure if we had room on our team. My team had filled up the fastest, everyone wanting an ex-pro player as their coach. The look in his eyes stopped me.

"This is important to you, huh, Cole?" I asked with a soft smile.

He nodded eagerly. "Yes. The thing is, he didn't sign up because he didn't think his uncle could afford it. His mom died and I guess that's why he can't pay, but he loves baseball more than anything."

My chest tightened. "Yes, absolutely, Cole," I said without another thought. "Tell him to come to the next practice."

There was no way I could let something as superficial as fees get in the way of a kid playing baseball. I knew exactly what it felt like to want to do something with every fiber of my being and not be able to. No kid should have to experience that. Especially one who seemed to be dealing with so much. I didn't know the details of Cole's friend's situation, but it seemed to me if baseball was something that could help him through a rough time, he needed it.

Cole rewarded me with a huge grin. "Thank you so much! You're the best coach ever!"

"Hey, what about your dear old dad?" Linc nudged Cole with his shoulder.

I laughed and pushed my chest out in mock pride. "What do you expect, Travers? You're up against me."

Cole grinned at our teasing, then got to work devouring the food that had arrived while we talked. Linc looked over at me and mouthed, *Thank you.*

I shrugged. It was nothing to thank me for. Helping kids discover their love for baseball had become my passion. Who was I to say no to letting his friend on the team? If I could do that small thing to help the boy, great. Maybe Cole thought that made me the best coach ever, but to me, it was just the right thing to do.

I may have had doubts about my ability to be the pack leader, but when it came to these kids, I had no doubts. I'd always do the right thing by them, no matter what.

Chapter 2 - Bryce

"Do you think she'll like the sunflowers, Uncle Bryce?" Liam looked up at me from the passenger seat of my truck, worry lines etching his forehead.

An eight-year-old boy shouldn't have worry lines. Hell, an eight-year-old boy shouldn't have to deal with any of what Liam had been through in the last six months.

I gave him a reassuring smile. "I know she'll love them. When your mother and I were little, she wanted a sunflower garden. Always talked about how they were her favorite flowers."

Liam's lips tipped up. "I didn't know that. Maybe I should have brought more. Made a little garden for her myself."

My shattered heart cracked a little more at his words. He was so innocent. So kind and caring. Lori had done an amazing job raising him. I didn't know how I would ever fill her shoes now she was gone.

"This is perfect," I told him, reaching over and squeezing his shoulder. "You ready?"

Liam took a tremulous breath, then nodded resolutely and climbed from my truck. Most days, he seemed to keep it together better than I did. Of course, he didn't have the overwhelming guilt of his mother's death resting on his shoulders.

By the time I managed to get my stiff legs out the door and lower myself to my feet, Liam was already on my side of the truck and reaching inside for my cane.

"Here you go, Uncle Bryce."

He had to be the most considerate kid I'd ever known. "Thanks, big guy."

I tried to suppress the wince of pain as I took a step forward, leaning heavily on my cane. My hips and legs were always extra tight when I'd been sitting for any length of time, and every step on my bad side sent shooting pain up through my back. The doctors and physical therapists said it would get better with time, though I may never walk completely normally again. Six months after the car accident, I was inclined to believe it.

Liam stayed right by my side as we made our way from the paved road that wound through the cemetery onto a dirt path that would lead us to my sister's grave. The ache in my hips was nothing compared to that of my heart.

People said the pain of losing my sister would ease with time as well. So far, that hadn't happened. Not when every time I thought of her, I replayed the accident in my mind, wondering what I could have done differently. If she would still be alive if I hadn't made the split-second decision that had caused the fatal crash.

Liam put his hand on my arm as we approached Lori's grave, as if he were the one giving me strength. This boy. He was something else. I'd never met a kinder soul in my life. I smiled, trying to be strong for him in return.

When we stopped in front of the small gravestone, Liam let go of my arm and stooped in front of the grave. He reached forward and brushed off some of the dirt that had gathered since we'd come last week. At first, I hadn't been sure it was a good idea to bring Liam here so regularly. I thought it might just lengthen the time it would take for him to heal, but it seemed to be good for him. Afterward he seemed a little more at ease, a little more at peace as if keeping a strong connection to his mother gave him the strength he needed to go on another week.

I swallowed hard as Liam cleared away the lilies we'd brought last week and replaced them with the vibrant sunflowers. It was fitting, as spring was just beginning to show its face in Timberwood Cove.

As I stood watching my nephew, a lump formed in my throat, only made worse when the faint strains of his little voice wafted toward me. Singing to his mother.

"You are my sunshine, my only sunshine…" He sang so softly and sweetly, his voice so full of love that it caused my chest to constrict.

It felt as if the weight of the world was on my shoulders. Liam was entirely my responsibility now, and I had to be strong for him. He needed me. Almost as much as I needed him. We were all each other had now. Liam had never known his father—he was the product of a one-night stand—but his mother had done more than double duty with parenting. She'd been the best mother any kid could ask for. It felt nearly impossible that I could be everything Liam needed now—but I was going to do my damnedest to try. It was the least I could do when it was my fault we were even in this position.

As Liam's song faded and he began to speak softly to his mother about what he'd been up to this week, my mind drifted back to the accident, as it always did.

The rainy road that wove through the forests north of Timberwood Cove. The fog on the road as the cool rain hit the pavement, still hot from an unusually hot fall day.

It was as if I were transported back to that moment. Looking over at Lori as she made some flippant comment about how we wouldn't have to be on the evening run into town to the hardware store in the first place if I'd remembered she needed me to replace some of the planks on her deck. I'd made some teasing remark, turning away from the road so she couldn't see me roll my eyes.

She's just shaken her head and laughed. That's how it had always been with Lori and me. We liked to give each other a hard time, but deep down neither of us ever took it seriously. We knew each other better than that—knew each other better than anyone. That's how it was with twins. There was a connection between them no one else could understand.

Which is probably why I hadn't been able to move on from that night. I'd lost the other half of my soul that night. How did you move on from something like that?

In my mind, I heard Lori's laugh cut off abruptly before she screamed my name.

"Bryce!" She'd thrown her arms out in front of her as a look of terror crossed her features, and I'd snapped my eyes back to the road.

Too late.

There, standing in the middle of the foggy road, illuminated by the beams of my headlights as we topped a hill, was a giant wolf, at least one and half times the size of any I'd ever seen before. It's green eyes glowed, catching in the headlights.

Not knowing what else to do, I'd swerved quickly to the left to avoid it. It had been an immediate reflex, no thought given to it. No thought given to the fact that I couldn't see over the top of the hill. Where a semi-truck was just appearing.

I swerved back to the right, right where the wolf was, and braced for impact. I didn't want to hit an innocent animal, but the alternative was colliding head-on with the truck.

It was too late, though. The last thing I remember was wondering where the wolf was, why I didn't see it standing in the road. Then the flash of headlights and the blare of a horn, mixing with Lori's scream before everything went black.

"Uncle Bryce?" Liam's little voice broke into my thoughts, jerking me out of the memory and back to the present. Tentatively, he added, "Are you okay?"

He looked up at me with a worried expression, and I wondered what I must look like in that moment. If the horror and guilt and pain were evident on my face. Quickly, I schooled my features, slipping on my mask I thought I'd nearly perfected. The impenetrable mask of strength I had to put on for Liam's sake.

"I'm okay," I said softly, forcing my mouth into a smile, though I wasn't sure it didn't look more like a grimace. In the wake of my memories, my legs were feeling weak, but I pushed down on my cane, standing taller and straightening my shoulders.

I had to be strong for him. I couldn't fall apart when so much was at stake. I was all he had left. Liam deserved the best life I could give him, and there was no room for weakness in my attempt to make that happen.

Liam turned back to the grave to tell his mother goodbye and that we'd be back next week with more updates.

"Maybe I'll have something exciting to tell you," he whispered. "Something I've been working on."

My eyes squeezed closed and I blew out a breath, reaching out to my twin myself now.

Please Lori. I need your help. I'm trying my best, but I worry it's not enough. Please give me the strength I need to raise your son to be the best person he can be. Then...then I'll be okay.

It wasn't about me anymore, though. Everything I did now was for Liam. Moving him from the town he and Lori and I had lived in to Timberwood Cove. Enrolling him in one of the best elementary schools around. Providing him more opportunities for a normal life than what we'd had before.

I couldn't think about what I needed outside of Liam. If I could just maintain the strength to be what he needed, I'd be fine. That would be enough to help me through my grief.

Liam pushed up from the ground and turned to me, reaching his hand out for my empty one, and we headed back toward the truck. My right leg was feeling stiff again, and I leaned on the cane as much as I could, trying not to let Liam see the struggle it was for me to make it back. He couldn't miss the limp, though.

I'd probably always have it.

Trying to draw attention away from my broken body, I glanced down at Liam. "What do you say we pick up some dinner on the way home?"

His eyes lit up. We never went out to dinner. It was hard enough to afford to keep us fed and clothed with a roof over our heads on the disability checks I now received—I'd been unable to continue in my trade after the accident. Yet one more thing I loved that had been ripped away in that fateful accident. It was hard to work construction when you could barely stand without help, much less climb a ladder or haul equipment around.

"Are you sure?" he asked me, biting his lower lip. "I mean, we don't have to."

God. This kid was forever selfless. He shouldn't have to worry about making ends meet. That was my job.

"Of course I'm sure," I said, forcing my voice to sound upbeat. "You deserve it, and if you eat some vegetables, I'll even get you some ice cream after?"

A smile spread across his face at that, and it made it more than worth it that I'd be eating peanut butter and jelly for lunch until the next check came in.

Once we got settled back in the car, Liam immediately flipped on the radio and tuned it to a sports station. He bounced up and down on the seat, pumping his fist in the air as he yelled out, "Yeah, they're in the lead!"

I had to laugh at his enthusiasm, and I felt the tightness in my chest loosen. Liam always had that effect on me, able to cheer me up and make me feel lighter.

"Is it the Timberwolves?" I asked, pulling the truck out onto Town Hall Road, heading toward the quaint downtown of Timberwood Cove. There were a lot of cute little restaurants along the street, but I continued past them. They were all above my price range.

"Yep," Liam said, beaming. "They're my favorite."

I chuckled. As if I didn't know that already. Liam lived and breathed the Takoma Timberwolves these days. He watched all the games—or listened to them when he couldn't, like right now—and brought home books from the library about his favorite team.

"Are they having a good season?" I asked, and Liam delved into all the stats from the season so far—though it was just beginning, he seemed to have it all figured out.

"They'll be at the World Series this year," he stated confidently. "Just you watch." He frowned a little. "Though they'd have a better chance if Jaxon Parsons was still on the team."

"Their old pitcher?" I asked, though I knew the answer. If the Timberwolves were Liam's favorite team, Jaxon Parsons was practically his idol.

He nodded, then he shot me a huge grin, his eyes lighting up like he'd just had an idea.

"Hey! I know we couldn't ever go to see a real game with the Timberwolves," he said, and my heart gave a heavy thud, realizing he meant we wouldn't ever have the money. "But my friend Cole at school plays baseball. He's in little league. First practice was today, in fact."

A flicker of sadness crossed his face, but it was gone almost before I'd seen it. I'd caught it, though. He wanted to play baseball just like his friend. I could practically read his thoughts; that he wouldn't even mention it to me, knowing we couldn't afford it.

I gripped the steering wheel a little tighter. I wanted to be able to give that to him. Baseball had become his passion, likely something that was helping him get through his grief of losing his mother, but we certainly didn't have the money to sign him up for little league, especially if we were splurging on going out to eat tonight.

And from the way it sounded, the little league season had already started.

"You and Cole seem to be pretty good friends," I commented. "I've heard you talk about him before."

Liam nodded vigorously. "My best friend."

Any tension I felt melted in that moment. Liam was doing better than I could expect, already making friends in a new school, which I knew had to be hard. Starting over in a new town, a new school, with a very different family dynamic than he'd had before, he seemed to be thriving. Well, as much as he could be, all things considered.

"So, what I was going to say, is that he'll be having some games soon, and I've never seen a real baseball game in person. Maybe we could go?" Liam looked at me hopefully.

There was no question. "Absolutely, big guy. You just let me know when, and we'll make it happen."

The excitement that spread over his face was all I needed. It gave me the strength to keep going. Knowing that there was a way for me to put that smile on his face got me through another day.

"Thanks, Uncle Bryce," he said, turning his attention back to the game.

We were nearing the edge of the tree-lined downtown street, and my eye caught on a little diner on the last corner.

The words *Kay's Diner* were lit up in neon on an old silver building. *Perfect,* I thought as I pulled into the parking lot. This looked like a fun place, and pretty affordable.

"Oh, I've heard about this place," Liam said. "Cole said it's one of his favorite restaurants."

I smiled, happy I'd decided to bring him out to eat. I hated that he probably always felt like he didn't have much compared to his friends. We rarely went out anywhere, he wore second-hand clothing, and lived in a tiny house near the school. I wished I could give him more.

After cutting off the ignition, I climbed out of the truck again, trying to move faster this time so Liam didn't feel as if he had to come help me. I barely leaned on the cane and focused my attention on walking with as little of a limp as possible.

Liam chattered on about going to see his friend's baseball game and what we might eat at the diner, but I was distracted by the wheels turning in my head. Was there a way I might be able to afford getting Liam in little league? There had to be.

I crunched the numbers in my head, calculating how much I'd have left in savings for next month's rent if I pulled some out to let him join. If it wasn't too late, that is.

My heart warmed just imagining the look on his face if I told him he got to play baseball just like Cole. It was enough to make me willing to figure it out. Somehow.

Liam ran ahead of me and opened the door to the diner, and I gave him a big grin as I lightly limped up to him, suppressing the wince of pain as I put more weight on my right leg instead of the cane.

"Aren't you the gentleman?" a woman said as she exited the diner, giving Liam an impressed little smile and pat on the head.

He beamed at her. "Just making my mom proud."

It felt as if the breath had been knocked out of me. In spite of the tragedy of our situation, I knew I couldn't be luckier to call this boy my nephew—and hopefully my son, soon, if everything with my case worker for Liam's adoption came through.

"She already is, big man," I said, walking into Kay's Diner and ruffling his hair myself. "She already is."

Chapter 3 - Jaxon

"Hope everything was good tonight," Kay said with a friendly smile as I handed her my check and credit card.

"Always," I said with a grin.

She nodded, satisfied. Kay always manned the front of her diner. It was part of the appeal. She knew everyone in town and always made them feel more than welcome. The food was pretty amazing too.

As she processed my payment for dinner, I glanced around the diner. Linc had headed to the restroom, and Cole was around here somewhere. As I turned, I caught a scent of something in the air.

Something like cedar, but with an edge to it I didn't recognize. Furrowing my brow, I looked around. There were no other shifters in the diner that I could sense. Just Linc and Cole.

What *was* that? I breathed in the scent, trying to place it. It drew me in, making me feel strangely captivated. I was curious to know who the source was of this distinctive scent. Suddenly, I remembered something about a fated mate's scent being unique and totally alluring. I shook my head, dazed. Was my mate seriously here right now?

As I carefully checked out the diner once more, I didn't see anything or anyone different, certainly no one who might be my mate. I pushed the thought away. I was probably just imagining it. Maybe the pressure I was feeling from my father wanting me to take over as pack leader had me jumping to conclusions, thinking that if I had my mate that was one less obstacle to overcome.

I was being ridiculous. I thanked Kay when she handed me my card and receipt, and then I turned toward the door. Cole was standing in the waiting area, talking with another boy his age. I guessed it was someone he knew from school. I strolled over to them while we waited for Linc to reappear. It didn't look like this kid's parents were anywhere to be seen.

"Hey," I said, slinging an arm around Cole's shoulders. "Who's your friend?"

The sandy blond-haired boy looked up at me, his eyes going wide. "Oh my gosh," he said, looking from me to Cole then back again. "You're Jaxon Parsons!"

I laughed and stuck out my hand. "That I am."

"You were Rookie of the Year, the best pitcher the entire major league had seen in years."

I chuckled again. It wasn't that often I ran into fans now I was back in Timberwood Cove, but it was always fun when they were kids.

"Sounds like you're a big baseball fan," I said.

"Big isn't the right word," he exclaimed, then he proceeded to rattle out stats from my entire career—something that had spanned more years than he'd been alive. He sounded so awestruck I was almost embarrassed. This kid didn't just sound like a baseball fan, but like the most well-informed sportscaster in history—one that specialized in me particularly.

I felt a little taken aback by how thorough his knowledge was. Sure, I had fans who knew all about my career, but this kid was something else.

He shook his head. "Mr. Parsons, you're my hero."

He said it so earnestly I couldn't help but feel humbled, but before I could say anything, Cole laughed and elbowed me in the side.

"Him? Nah, he's just Jaxon, my dad's best friend. This is my friend Liam I was telling you about."

Cole had neglected to mention the kid was a super fan.

"Your dad's best friend?" Liam looked at me in awe again.

I grinned as he finally shook my outstretched hand. "Nice to meet you, Liam."

He practically glowed. "This is incredible! Wait until I tell my uncle!"

Just then I caught that scent again—cedar mingled with something unfamiliar. Stronger this time. I turned my attention from the boys back toward the counter, where a man was making his way between some tables toward the waiting area.

Holy. Fuck.

The scent hit me harder, coming in waves from the man who was grimacing as he leaned on a cane. However, that wasn't what really caught my attention. My gaze became transfixed on the man's face. The angular line of his jaw, his roman nose, his full lips, the dark blond hair falling over narrow eyes.

He was sexy as hell.

I felt my wolf spring to life in the back of my mind. Apparently he recognized the scent as well. Instinct kicked in, and I started toward the stranger before I even knew what was happening. I was drawn to him—pulled, as if there was something binding us together. Was he my mate?

Just as the enormity of that possibility set in, the bottom of the man's cane got caught on a chip in the tile floor, and his leg suddenly gave out. He began to stumble and fall. I darted forward as fast as I could, but I was too late, and he landed hard on his side.

The sounds in the diner came to a screeching halt, everyone turning to see what had just happened.

"Are you okay?" I asked as I reached his side, the scent of him nearly overpowering now. When I touched his arm, he jerked his head up to me, and for a minute I was captured in the intensity of his piercing hazel eyes.

He tightened his jaw, and his cheeks turned red as he glanced around the diner, realizing everyone was staring at him. I looked up at the other diners, narrowing my gaze, feeling an urge to protect this man from their prying eyes; and everyone looked away. The din picked up again, a bit softer now, but I tuned it all out, dropping my gaze and focusing on this beautiful man.

He was already pushing himself up, not looking at me now. "I'm fine." But his voice sounded strained as he got to his knees and reached for his cane.

"Here, let me help you," I said quickly, reaching to grasp him around his waist. I accidentally brushed my fingers against his arm and felt a spark of nerves, a rush of awareness where my skin touched his. He didn't seem to notice.

"Are you okay?" I asked again, once he was on his feet.

His mouth stretched into a line, and I wasn't sure if it was a smile or a grimace.

"Yes," he said, his voice a little rough. "I said I was fine."

I glanced over at Kay. "He needs a table."

Without waiting for a response I helped the man over to the nearest booth. It was obvious he needed my assistance but was trying his hardest not to lean on me. He put his weight into the cane and limped a few steps until we were at the booth.

"Uncle Bryce! Are you okay?" The little boy who Cole had been talking with came rushing over to us, looking worried as he searched the man's face.

I felt an immediate shift in the man. He stood straighter, squaring his shoulders, and smiled at Liam.

My stomach did a little flip. Even though I could tell the smile was forced, the way his eyes lit up as he looked at the boy only made me want to see more of that smile.

Cole ran up to join us as the man lowered himself into the booth. I reluctantly drew my hand away. I couldn't exactly stand there with my hands all over a man I'd never met, even though my wolf clawing at my mind seemed to want me to do just that.

"Liam, is this your uncle?" Cole asked, looking between the two of them.

"Yeah, this is my Uncle Bryce."

Bryce.

I wanted to slide right into the booth next to him. Instead I just extended my hand to him like I had to Liam.

"Hey, Bryce. I'm Jaxon."

When he shook my hand, I felt that same spark radiating up my arm, and that's when I knew. Liam's uncle was my fated mate.

I blew out a breath in both shock and joy. My mate! I'd found him!

He looked up at me, those hazel eyes locking with mine again, and he gave me a small smile. Not as bright as the one he gave his nephew, but at least this smile was directed at me.

"Nice to meet you. And, uh…thanks for the help." He looked away then, like he was embarrassed about the fall. I didn't give a fuck about that, though. I just wanted to make sure he was okay.

"Is there anything you need?" He frowned and shook his head, but before he could say anything, I put up my hand. "Hang on, I'll be right back."

Linc had just caught my attention at the front of the restaurant. I gave him a wave then walked back to the counter where Kay was closing out another patron's check. I heard Liam and Cole talking over the din of the other diners, no doubt because I was tuning every heightened sense I had toward their table.

I smiled as I heard Liam telling his uncle that I was Jaxon Parsons, his favorite baseball player *ever*. Then I stepped up to Kay and leaned over the counter.

"Kay, I want to prepay for their meal. Whatever they want, it's on me," I said, handing her my credit card again.

As she ran my card for the second time, I started thinking about what Cole had said earlier. This must be the friend he was talking about who wanted to play ball with him but didn't have the money.

"Anything they want," I reiterated to Kay as she handed me a blank receipt and I signed my name. I felt the overwhelming urge to make sure Bryce and Liam were taken care of tonight. It was just something small, but if they were struggling, I wanted to help.

I headed right back over to the table, ignoring the look Linc gave me from where he was waiting at the front door. When I came to stand at the table again, it took everything I had in me to keep myself in control. I wanted to reach over and brush the blond hair off Bryce's forehead. Run my fingers along his jaw, over his lips…

My wolf was going crazy, but I forced myself to put on the appearance of being a perfect gentleman. To not reveal the very dirty thoughts that were swiftly going through my mind. Despite that, I couldn't tear my eyes away from him. He looked up at me as if he felt the intensity of my gaze, a line forming between his eyebrows. Did he feel this too? Was it just me? Was I the only one having this reaction because he was my mate? I studied him, looking for some sign that he was conscious of the undeniable awareness channeling between us.

But he didn't appear fazed at all. Of course not. Why would he? He was human.

That was something I hadn't thought about at first, my mind so filled with the knowledge that I'd found my mate—and more than a little distracted by the pure sexiness he radiated. As a human he wouldn't be aware of the concept of fated mates—hell, chances were he wasn't even aware of the existence of shifters.

Still looking at Bryce, I said, "Liam, I have a great idea."

With what felt like superhuman effort, I dragged my gaze from Bryce and focused on the boy. "Why don't you come join the team at our next practice? We could use someone who knows baseball as well as you."

Liam practically came out of his seat. "Are you serious?" he asked, lighting up as only little kids could.

"No—um—I—" Bryce's voice brought me right back to staring at him. He cleared his throat. "What I mean is, I'm not sure…"

I saw a muscle in his jaw tick with tension. His shoulders seemed to drop slightly as he looked over at Liam, who was now looking guiltily at his uncle. I could tell that the next thing Bryce said was incredibly painful, even though he tried to cover it with a smile for Liam.

"Thank you, but I'm afraid that's an expense we just can't afford right now. We have some things…going on."

Liam's shoulders deflated, but he didn't say anything. Just reached out and wordlessly squeezed his uncle's hand.

It nearly broke my heart.

"No, no," I said quickly, already having made my decision even before meeting both uncle and nephew. "Don't worry about anything like that. I've got it all covered. We have plenty of equipment, and if Liam needs a ride to practice, we can handle that too."

Bryce opened his mouth to protest, and I could see he didn't like the idea of someone giving them what probably equated to a handout in his mind. Even though I didn't know him, I could read the pride and determination clearly on his face.

I cut him off before he could object, though. "Seriously. I insist. In fact, I wouldn't have it any other way. I meant it when I said we could use a kid like Liam on the team. His enthusiasm enough will be exactly what the other kids need."

I leaned over the table, grabbed a napkin and a pen a server must have left behind, and then scribbled my number down.

"Liam, here's my number," I said, passing the boy the napkin. My eyes never left Bryce, and I hoped the insistence in my gaze made it clear I really wouldn't take no for an answer. "Next practice is Tuesday evening. Let me know if you need a ride."

Bryce looked at me, something like relief and resignation on his face. He looked like he was struggling with what to say, and I wondered how I must appear to him. Probably like an alpha getting turned on by a totally sexy omega. Surely it wasn't the first time he'd been stared at that way, but as I continued to gaze at him I saw a flush creep up his neck. My body immediately reacted to it, my cock twitching to life. Fuck. I really didn't need to sport a boner right here in front of the entire diner, but it was impossible to deny how he was affecting me. How the air between us seemed to thicken.

"Thank you," he finally said, giving me a genuine smile.

That smile nearly undid me, and I found myself grinning back, leaning in a little closer.

"Yes, thank you so much!" Liam declared, reminding me that we were indeed surrounded by other people.

I turned to him, making myself look away from Bryce. "Make sure you get dessert, okay? I'll see you two at the ball field next week then." Then I turned back to Bryce. "Remember all you have to do is call if you need anything. Like a ride, I mean."

Though I really meant if he needed anything at all. The need to look out for Bryce and Liam suddenly felt as natural as breathing. Bryce simply nodded, his brow furrowing again, and I knew I had to go now before I did something crazy without thinking. He already looked unsettled.

"Let's go, Cole. Your dad is waiting."

I headed toward the front of the restaurant, leaving Cole to say his goodbyes. Every step I took I became more and more aware of a string of energy connecting me right back to where Bryce sat. Yes, he was definitely my mate.

I grinned at the thought.

"What the fuck are you smiling at?" Linc asked me as we made our way out the door. He waved back to Cole. "Come on, buddy."

Cole loped after us as we climbed into my car so I could take them back to the ball field where they could get theirs to go home.

Linc looked at me expectantly. "What was that all about?"

I settled behind the wheel then turned to him. "That man is my fated mate."

Astonishment crossed Linc's face for only a moment before he grinned like a big idiot, just as I certainly was.

"Dude! That's amazing!" He turned in his seat to look back at the diner, like he could see Bryce inside. "That guy with Liam?"

Cole jumped in the back and leaned forward between the front seats, apparently having heard what I said.

"Liam's uncle is your mate?" he asked at practically the top of his voice, his eyes as wide as Liam's had been when he'd seen me in the diner.

Linc and I laughed at his enthusiasm.

"You can't go around saying that," Linc said with a wink.

"That means Liam will end up being part of our pack." Cole pumped his fist in the air. "This is awesome!"

I smiled, even though Cole was getting way ahead of himself, but his excitement was contagious because he was right. Bryce was my mate, so both him and Liam would be welcomed into the pack with open arms.

The fact that he was a human made things a little more complicated, and I realized I'd have to really be careful to handle this the right way. Not only would he be learning that I was a shifter, but we were fated to be together. I didn't have the faintest clue how that would play out, which was why I wasn't still in the diner, divulging everything to Bryce and asking if I could go home with him.

I needed to court him. Get him to like me, fall in love with me, and only then could I tell him who I was. I smiled again, thrilled about finally finding my fated mate. And he was literally the sexiest man I'd ever seen.

Chapter 4 - Bryce

"Jaxon Parsons!" Liam exclaimed for what had to be the hundredth time since we left Kay's Diner. He bounced up and down on his bed, eyes shining. "Can you believe it? He's the nicest ever!"

I chuckled. Jaxon Parsons indeed. He did seem to be quite the man, in more ways than I was sure I wanted to contemplate. Just the fact that he'd insisted Liam play on the team regardless of our ability to pay spoke volumes about the type of person he was.

Listening to Liam talk about how he got to play baseball on none other than his hero's little league team made me feel a rush of gratitude. I wondered if that had been evident in my thanks to Jaxon at the restaurant. I was pretty sure it wasn't. My thanks may even have come off begrudgingly, but it was only because I'd been caught up in a mix of anxiety and embarrassment at having to admit I couldn't afford for Liam to play. Yet Jaxon had brushed over that fact smoothly, as if it didn't even matter. It seemed like the only thing that mattered was Liam being able to play ball. Jaxon had been so insistent. So in control of the entire situation.

I was pretty sure I wouldn't have been able to say no to him even if Liam's happiness weren't part of the equation.

"Tuesday is forever away, Uncle Bryce," he said now, his face going from joyful to despondent in a matter of seconds.

I laughed again. "It will be here soon enough. Even sooner if you get to sleep. It's past your bedtime, big man."

Liam flopped back on his pillow, and I reached to pull the blankets up over him. "I still can't believe it."

"Well, believe it," I said with a smile. "It's happening. You're going to be a baseball player."

It was really more than I could even hope to ask for. Liam got to do what he'd been longing to, and it wouldn't affect the budget. On the one hand, it kind of felt like a handout, and that was something that rubbed me the wrong way, but at the same time, Jaxon hadn't made it seem like that at all. He'd seemed completely sincere in his claims that the team needed Liam.

"Thank you so much for letting me do this," Liam said.

I felt my chest tighten. "We really need to be thanking Mr. Parsons."

Liam nodded. "Maybe we could write a thank you note."

As usual, this kid shocked me with his kindness and thoughtfulness. "That sounds like a great idea," I said, leaning over to brush Liam's shaggy blond hair off his forehead and press a soft kiss there. "Let's do it tomorrow."

I stood from his bed and switched off the lamp on his bedside table. "Sweet dreams."

"You too, Uncle Bryce." His little voice followed me as I headed out of his room, a smile still on my face.

I had to admit, I couldn't wait until Tuesday either. Knowing I'd see Jaxon again. I wondered if he'd look at me the way he had before, with such intensity in his gaze. My body felt warm all over again when I thought about it. I didn't understand it, but I could have sworn there was something there between us.

My attraction to him was undeniable. He had to be one of the sexiest men I'd ever seen. That dark hair, longer on top with waves that kept falling over his forehead. The piercing green eyes. His strong jaw and full lips.

I groaned. I really didn't need to be thinking about how sexy my nephew's new baseball coach was, but I couldn't seem to get the image of him out of my head. His broad shoulders and lean torso, the strength that was visible in his hard, muscular biceps.

I wasn't sure if I'd imagined it or what, but I could have sworn there was something even more than attraction flowing between us. I felt almost drawn to him, like I needed to know him. I didn't understand that at all, but I'd also never been more intrigued by someone than I was by Jaxon.

I needed to get to bed soon too. My body was still aching from my fall, and I knew tomorrow would be an even harder day if I didn't get a good night's sleep. I headed to my bedroom, and then emptied my pockets onto my dresser before starting to strip. As I tossed my shirt aside, the breeze it created caused something on my dresser to flutter.

The napkin Jaxon had written his number down on. I'd stuffed it into my pocket earlier. I reached for it, studying the bold scrawl, and I felt an overwhelming urge to call him. Just to hear his smooth baritone. A shiver raced through my body just thinking about it.

Yeah, no. That was definitely a bad idea. I'd probably just end up sounding stupid. Walking into the bathroom to brush my teeth, I thought back over our exchange and wondered again if I hadn't seemed grateful enough.

I wanted him to know how much I appreciated what he was doing for Liam. Finishing up in the bathroom, I returned to my bedroom and shut the door but didn't climb straight into bed. I went to my dresser again and fingered the napkin.

Before I knew what I was doing, I had my phone in my hand, inputting his number into a text.

I bit my lip and thought about what I should say. I wanted to thank him, of course, but I didn't want to come off as over-eager, either. I had to make sure it was professional, not a hint of my personal feelings toward him shining through in case I'd imagined the way I thought he looked at me.

I typed out three different messages and erased them all before finally settling on something.

Hey, this is Bryce. Just wanted to let you know Liam is over the moon. Thank you again.

I pushed send before I could think better of it. Almost immediately, a text pinged back. My heart drummed a hasty beat as I opened the message.

The pleasure is all mine. Hope to see you soon.

I swallowed, a smile creeping over my face. I didn't want to read into it too much, but he'd said he hoped to see *me* soon. Maybe he was just using the general you, referring to both Liam and me.

I set my phone down and sat on the edge of my bed, the image of Jaxon's face still floating in my mind as I began to carefully remove my jeans. I winced at the stiffness in my hips and lower back. Lying down, I settled myself comfortably and drew in some deep breaths, going through the relaxation techniques I'd been practicing, trying to loosen up my stiff muscles before drifting off. I would definitely be hurting tomorrow. I couldn't believe I'd been such an idiot, falling right there in the middle of the restaurant.

I should have been humiliated by it—I'd definitely worried about embarrassing Liam, but Jaxon hadn't made me feel badly about it. In fact, he'd been incredibly sweet, and one look from him got all the other diners' attention off me.

He'd been so...gentle. So caring and sincere. The way my body had reacted to his hands on mine had been nothing less than shocking. Like a current of electricity had flowed from his body right into mine, lighting me up from the inside out.

Even thinking about it now, lying in bed, my pulse raced. He'd been so attentive, so charming, so very...alpha. He practically oozed a sense of control. A man who knew what he wanted and wouldn't take no for an answer. The omega in me responded to it immediately.

I groaned as I brushed my hand down over the sheets. Fuck. My dick was getting hard just thinking about him. God, I hoped he hadn't seen I was having the same response to him when we were at the diner.

Blowing out a deep breath, I willed myself to stop thinking about him and return to my relaxation routine. Yeah fucking right. Not happening. Not with the raging boner I was now sporting. There was only one way I'd be getting to sleep now.

My dick seemed thrilled by the idea when I pulled the sheet down and wrapped my fist around it. It swelled and jerked in my hand, and another groan escaped my lips.

Jaxon's arms came to mind almost immediately. Those large biceps that were practically bulging with barely contained strength.

Closing my eyes, I pumped my cock faster, imagining it was Jaxon's hand wrapped around me, stroking me from base to tip, his fingers working me over as he built up my pleasure.

Pleasure...

I let myself imagine those words falling from Jaxon's lips, his voice husky with desire.

The pleasure is all mine, he'd said.

I bit my lip, my balls tightening, and I reached down to tease them with my other hand. Jolts of heat begin radiating through my body, pulsing out from a tingling in my spine until I felt like every nerve was blazing.

My breath hitched, my pulse raced, and my body thrummed as I continued to stroke myself higher and higher. In my mind, I saw the way Jaxon looked at me as he'd scribbled his number down on the napkin. The way his eyes had cut right through me, unsettling me and exciting me at the same time.

Then that smile he'd given me before he left...

With a strangled shout, I tightened my fist around my cock as my orgasm hit me hard. I felt it in my entire body. Intense waves of pleasure rocketing through me as my cock throbbed, hot cum spurting out to land on my bare stomach. I bit down harder on my lip as I rode the wave, my body jerking with every pulse.

Aftershocks wracked me, and I drew in a ragged breath, slowly opening my eyes. Holy shit. That was one of the most intense orgasms I'd ever had, just from pleasuring myself. I couldn't even imagine what it would be like if I were experiencing the real deal and not just fantasizing about Jaxon.

My heart still raced and I tried to get my breathing under control. I would definitely sleep better now, at least. My body felt limp, completely relaxed.

But as I slowly came back to reality from my hot little fantasy, I realized I was kidding myself. Why the hell would a wealthy former pro baseball player ever be interested in a guy like me? Someone who was disabled, broke, struggling to make it day to day. An omega who had the huge responsibility of taking care of a young boy on top of it.

I swallowed hard. He wouldn't. My imagination must have been working overtime at the diner, my inexplicable draw to Jaxon coloring my memories of him.

I had to remember who he was. Who I was. Because I'd be seeing him again in just a few days and didn't need to make a fool of myself. Still, it didn't stop me from thinking of him as I finally drifted off to sleep.

***

"Come on, Liam, we're already late," I called through the bathroom door.

The last five days had dragged on, but finally it was Tuesday evening and time for Liam's first practice with Jaxon's little league team. And of course, we were running behind.

Dinner had taken longer than I meant it to. It had been a hard day with an uncomfortable amount of pain, and prolonged standing had taken its toll on me.

"Coming!" he called back, his voice sounding worried. "Do you think they'll still let me be on the team if we're late?"

"Yeah, big man, don't worry about that," I said, my stomach dropping that he'd even think such a thing, and that my shortcomings were what had caused it in the first place. Just then, I heard a knock on the front door. Great. What now?

I rushed to look through the peephole, and my stomach sank even further. Fuck, what was she doing here?

I opened the door quickly, swallowing my anxiety and trying to put on a confident air. "Mrs. Pinder," I said. "I wasn't expecting you."

She looked at me over the top of her thick glasses, studying me like she was trying to find something to fault me for. Wasn't she supposed to be on my side? She was Liam's caseworker, and should know the right thing was for me to adopt him, yet she always made me feel like she thought differently.

"May I come in?" she asked, pursing her lips and looking over my shoulder like she wanted to find evidence that my home was unsuitable.

I remained in the doorway, not wanting to let her in on sheer principle. She shouldn't be showing up here unexpectedly. "We were actually just leaving. In fact, we're going to be late if we don't go now."

She narrowed her eyes like I'd said the wrong thing. "This is very important, Mr. Baldwin. I've been trying to get your financial information for days now."

Fuck. I'd been so preoccupied with making ends meet I'd forgotten she asked for my financials last week. I raked my hand through my hair and gave her a tight smile.

"Yes, I'm sorry. Perhaps we can schedule a better time when we aren't due to be somewhere."

"I'm ready now!" Liam said, darting into the room with a baseball hat in one hand and a glove and ball in the other. Cole had lent them to him last Friday at school so he could practice. Unfortunately, he'd been on his own there. I'd been in too much pain to even throw a ball around with him.

I turned to face him. "Yes, I just need to speak to Mrs. Pinder for a moment to schedule an appointment."

She must have taken that as an invitation because she stepped inside and shut the door behind her. "Mr. Baldwin, I need to see proof of your annual income and household expenses if you want to move forward with the adoption case."

I ground my teeth together, trying not to let my frustration show, but I could feel the tension radiating down my spine, my shoulders tensing as my legs clenched. I had to lean more heavily on the cane, something that didn't escape the social worker's sharp eyes.

"Hmm," she said. "I'm sorry, but this just can't wait."

I sighed, not sure how I could get out of this right now. I definitely didn't want to get into a confrontation with the woman who held the power to determine mine and Liam's future.

Liam came up and tugged my arm, his eyes full of worry. "We have to go."

"I know that, Liam. Just give me a minute. Please." Though I'd tried to soften my voice, I knew I sounded harsh, my agitation at Mrs. Pinder's unwarranted intrusion impossible to censor. She was totally out of line here, and I needed to apologize to Liam the second this woman was out the door.

Her lips pressed into a flat line, her eyes widening as she looked between Liam's desperate face and my stiff stance. "Mr. Baldwin, I'm highly concerned about Liam's wellbeing."

Fuck. Now I was digging myself into an even deeper hole with her. I didn't know what to say. If she was really concerned with Liam's wellbeing she would recognize how important is was for him to get to baseball practice instead of holding us hostage here.

"Your stress level only seems to increase every time I see you, Mr. Baldwin. With this shortness and irritability, combined with your disability and illness, I'm really starting to worry that you can handle the stresses involved in raising a child."

Okay. That was it. I wasn't going to have this woman stand here in my house and tell me that my stress was affecting my ability to handle Liam—when she was the one causing the stress in the first place.

Determination to get Liam to practice gave me the courage I needed to put things back on an even footing. I moved to the door and opened it, turning and looking back at her meaningfully.

"Mrs. Pinder, I'm going to have to ask you to leave. If you want to make an appointment to go over my financial situation, we can do that tomorrow. Right now, we have somewhere to be." My voice sounded stronger this time, firmer, but she didn't seem to like that any better than my earlier frustration. "I need to get Liam to the baseball field for practice."

She stepped toward me, glancing out the door before she looked back to me. "Fine," she huffed. "But I can't reiterate enough the importance of you getting me proof that you can care for Liam financially."

A quick intake of breath had me turning to look through the open door… To find Jaxon standing on my front porch.

Dammit. Could this day get any worse? I didn't know how much Jaxon had heard of that little exchange. He already knew we couldn't afford baseball, now he'd probably be wondering just how bad things were. A heated flush of embarrassment rose on my neck.

"I was just coming by to see if Liam was coming to practice tonight," he said. He was studying me closely, and I felt even more embarrassed that he'd caught me here with the social worker discussing my money—or lack thereof.

Instead of seeing any judgment in his gaze as he looked between Mrs. Pinder and me, he looked...upset. A mixture of concern, frustration, and irritation. I didn't know what to make of that, but Mrs. Pinder drew my attention back to her with her next words.

"You need to be aware, Mr. Baldwin, that it may be a hard battle to adopt Liam. Your cooperation would be greatly appreciated." Then she swept through the door, her gaze narrowed on Jaxon, but she didn't say anything to him. Not even a hello. What a bitch.

When she was in her car and out of earshot, Jaxon gave me a tentative smile, though I could see the tension in his shoulders. "I'm sorry to just show up like this. I was just concerned when Liam wasn't at practice after I'd insisted. Seriously, Bryce, we want him on the team."

"We were just running late," Liam interjected.

I rested my hand on his shoulder. "That would be my fault. I'm sorry, Jaxon." I gave him an apologetic smile. "We really do appreciate what you're doing, and there's no way we'd miss practice. I'm so sorry we got held up. I really did have every intention of having Liam there on time."

Jaxon's tentative smile widened into a pleased grin. "Good," he murmured. "Hey, why don't I give Liam a ride? You could join us, and maybe get dinner after?"

Well, that wasn't what I expected. I wanted nothing more than to spend a little more time with this man who'd been caring enough to come over and check on Liam, obviously leaving baseball practice to do so.

A *yes* was on my lips, but as I stepped back to let Jaxon in the door, my right leg gave out and I started to stumble. Just like in the diner. I was about to make a fool of myself in front of him yet again.

Instead of falling to the ground like I had before, I found myself being caught up in his arms, his movements swift and sure. The strength of his grip around me had my breath hitching, and when I looked up at him, I could have sworn I saw something in his eyes.

The same thing I'd managed to convince myself I'd imagined at the diner five days ago. Attraction. Curiosity. Intrigue. But there was something else there now. Something I recognized well because I was feeling it just as strongly...

Desire.

Chapter 5 - Jaxon

My entire body tuned into Bryce as I held him in my arms. Electricity crackled through my veins. The air between us thickened, and as I stared down at him, I knew he felt it too. I could see the same desire coursing through me reflected in the hazel depths of his eyes.

My wolf reared up inside me, clawing at me to get out. I was barely in control, especially when Bryce's lips fell open as he sucked in a ragged breath. My gaze fell to his mouth, and all I wanted in that moment was to taste him. To feel those lips beneath my own. To fucking *do something* about this burning need inside me that demanded I make him *mine*.

Trying to steady myself, I helped Bryce regain his balance, and then I stepped back.

"Um," Bryce said breathlessly, his eyes locked on mine. He seemed at a loss for words. He licked his lips nervously; and seeing the pink tip of his tongue had all kinds of dangerous ideas forming in my mind. Then he blinked.

"Thank you. I don't know what happened there." He dropped his gaze and looked away, his mouth forming a thin line.

"Don't even think twice about it," I said quickly. The last thing I wanted was Bryce pulling away after I'd felt that connection sparking to life between us, but that's just what he did.

He turned and took an unsteady step toward the living room. "Thanks for coming by to check on Liam," he said over his shoulder.

"Would you like to come with us?" I asked again, coming up to his side in case his leg gave out on him. "I'll drive."

Bryce shook his head. "That sounds great but…" He blew out a breath and grimaced. "I'm not even sure I should leave the house now. I've had a bit of a flare-up today, and this whole thing didn't help any."

He must have meant the exchange I'd caught the tail end of between him and that social worker. I wanted to question him, to find out more about what was going on, wanting to do whatever I could to help make things easier for him and Liam. My wolf practically demanded I did. The urge to protect was so strong I didn't know what to make of it, other than knowing this was how things were between mates—that an alpha went to any length for his omega.

"Okay," I said, though I didn't feel okay about leaving him here at all. "I'll just take Liam to practice and then bring him back when we're done. Is there anything I can do for you, though?"

I placed my hand on his forearm, and Bryce looked up at me. There it was again. That sizzling heat between us. He had to feel something, even if he didn't recognize what I was to him.

"I just need to get settled. I'm sorry, Liam," he said, turning his attention to the worried little boy. "You go along with Jaxon and I'll be fine, okay?"

Liam nodded, though he still looked concerned.

I gave him a smile and dug my keys out of my pocket. "Why don't you go pick out a bat that you like from my car? I'll just get your uncle taken care of and be right out."

I was rewarded with a giant grin, then Liam was snatching the keys and racing out of the house.

I chuckled. "He's a good kid."

Bryce nodded, his expression softening, the tension that had been there before melting as he watched his nephew run off. "That he is." He looked back at me, and some of the tension fell back into place. "I'm fine. You go on."

No way. I wasn't leaving him here like this, not knowing if he would make it through the house without another fall.

"It's no problem," I said, leading him over to the couch in the tiny cracker box of a living room. I wrapped my arm around his waist to help him down onto it and felt that energy race up my arm yet again.

He sank into the cushions, looking up at me, but I didn't let go of him immediately, resting my hand on his shoulder. More than anything, I wanted to trace the curve of his neck up to that sharp jaw, then run my fingers along his lips.

The air thickened once more, full of an awareness that there was something very real between us even though we'd only just met. I was pretty sure he felt it too, though I knew he didn't understand its source.

Reluctantly, I pulled my hand away. "Get some rest, okay? I'll bring some food back for you later."

A smile threatened, his lips curving slightly, and I liked knowing I put it there.

"Thank you," he said yet again.

I shook my head. "No thanks needed." Then, before I gave in to my instincts and found out exactly what that mouth tasted like, I stepped back. "See you later."

I felt his gaze on me as I turned and walked out of the house. Liam was already in the passenger seat, bouncing up and down as he held one of my favorite old bats in his hands.

I chuckled as I climbed into the car and revved the engine. "That's a good one. Sturdy and solid. Nice choice."

He beamed at me for a moment, but as I pulled out onto Poplar Road and headed toward the sports complex, I felt Liam shift and glance at me. He only hesitated a moment before diving right into what was on his mind.

"I'm worried about that woman," he blurted out.

I tore my gaze from the road just long enough to make out the worry lines marring his forehead. I didn't know what to say. I didn't want to pry, and I didn't know the full details of the situation.

"She said it was going to be hard for Uncle Bryce to adopt me. Every time he meets with her, it just upsets him. I don't know what to do. I don't want to go into foster care."

It hurt my heart that he was so troubled over this. Without even thinking about what I was saying, just following my gut, I told him, "You don't have to worry about that, Liam. Seriously. I won't let that happen. I'll take care of everything."

He blinked, a little taken aback, but a tentative smile began to form. "You've always been my hero, Jaxon," he said, somewhat in awe.

I chuckled. "Well, I don't know about that, but I can promise you I'll come through for you here." And I meant it with very fiber of my being. I was meant to take care of Bryce—and Liam too.

"How can you be so sure, though?" Liam asked. "How can you say that when you barely even know me or my uncle?"

Such a level-headed little boy. He'd been through so much already in his young life. Probably not really getting to be a kid because he'd been so wrapped up in the adult worries surrounding him.

I wanted to reassure him there was nothing that could keep me from taking care of them, but I didn't know how without revealing the connection I already had to his uncle, to my mate—or the fact that I was a shifter. So I left it alone for now, telling him again not to worry about it, to just enjoy the practice that awaited us.

We didn't have long for conversation anyway, as I was already pulling into the sports complex. Practice was already in full-swing—I'd told Linc to get started without me when I'd realized Liam wasn't there at the beginning and I'd felt the irrepressible need to go check on them.

It didn't seem to faze Liam, though. He was just thrilled to be here. He darted out onto the field to join the team, knowing where to go without me even telling him. He knew baseball, that was for sure. I couldn't wait to see him out there playing.

Following him out to the field, I dove in, losing myself in the rush I got any time I was on a ball field. Practice flew by, and I loved every minute of it. Even though I was completely immersed in my role as coach, giving all the kids my attention as needed, I couldn't help watching Liam in particular.

He really did have natural talent. He wasn't just a fan. It amazed me when he told me he had never really played before. A swell of pride filled my chest as I watched him. It was almost like seeing a younger version of myself, his passion for the game so raw and unfiltered.

By the time practice was over and all the kids were getting their equipment packed up, I couldn't wait to get back to Bryce's and tell him all about it, but Cole and Liam were quick to remind me we were supposed to go get dinner.

I laughed. "I think you guys worked up quite an appetite." I handed a bag of baseballs to them. "Here, go pack this up in my car and we can get going."

"That kid's a natural," Linc remarked as they hurried away.

"Right? I thought so too," I replied, watching them as they loped over to my car and hefted the bag into the trunk. Then I turned to Linc. "When I went to pick Liam up, I spoke to Bryce again."

"Yeah? Did you kiss him?"

"No." I shook my head, suppressing a grin at Linc's interest in my love life. "Not yet."

"Well don't wait too long. If I found my fated mate I'd be all over him."

I laughed. "I'm sure you would."

"Yeah, maybe, but because of Cole I think I've left it too late. I doubt I'll find my mate now."

"I wouldn't be too sure. I thought the same thing, but then Bryce literally fell into my life." And because of his disability, he couldn't be here now.

"So why the frown?" Linc asked.

I sighed. "There are…obstacles," I said, thinking about Liam and what he said about the social worker and his fear of being put into foster care.

"Whatever it is, you can handle it," Linc said, his faith in me making me smile again.

I nodded. "Yeah. I will," I said with resolve. Because I knew I'd stop at nothing to make sure Bryce and Liam were taken care of and that we could be together. I'd figure it all out, somehow.

The boys decided on Kay's Diner for dinner again—and they got no arguments from me. The hour passed by in loud, boisterous conversation and laughter, and just before we finished up, I ordered a meal for Bryce.

Linc gave me a knowing grin and a wink, and I couldn't suppress the thrill that went through me knowing I was about to head back over and see Bryce again. After that, I couldn't get out of there fast enough. We'd taken separate cars this time since I had Liam with me, and the boys said their goodbyes before we took off.

When we pulled back up at Bryce's house, I barely kept myself from flying out of the car and up the steps. Instead, I let Liam lead the way.

Inside, we found Bryce still on the couch where I'd left him.

"Hey, big man," Bryce said smiling, though I could see he was still in pain by the stiffness in his body. "How was practice?"

"You've got quite the ball player on your hands, Bryce," I said, sitting down next to him on the couch and placing the bag of take-out food on the coffee table.

Liam went immediately into a play-by-play of the entire practice, his excitement radiating from his beaming face. I couldn't stop grinning as I listened while I took Bryce's dinner from the bag and started arranging it on the plate Kay had provided.

Bryce kept shooting me glances, watching me out of the corner of his eye as he listened to Liam. I turned and smiled at him, handing him the plate. Our gazes caught, and I felt that awareness race through me once again, a feeling I was starting to identify as my wolf recognizing him as my mate.

"Thank you," he said, taking the plate.

"You have to come next time, Uncle Bryce," Liam said, just before a huge yawn took hold of his little body.

Bryce chuckled, a smooth sound that pulsed through me. "I'll be there. I need to see you in action for myself, but for now, I think you need to head off to bed. It's getting late."

He started to push forward on the couch, setting his plate back on the table, and I saw him wince, though he tried to hide it.

"You know what?" I pushed the plate back into his hands. "You stay here and eat, and I'll see Liam off to bed. If he's lucky, I might just tell him an old baseball tale for a bedtime story."

Liam leaped up at that. "I'm gonna go brush my teeth!"

I laughed. "That okay with you?" I asked Bryce when Liam bounded out of the room. I didn't want to cross any lines, even though to me, it felt perfectly natural to think about taking care of Liam. It was amazing how quickly I was feeling protective of both of them.

Bryce nodded and opened his mouth to say something, but I held a hand up and laughed again. "I'm going to say it one more time. No need for thanks."

I followed after Liam, and true to my word, regaled him with one of my old baseball stories, one from my rookie year. He listened raptly, but before long was drifting off.

Standing, I flipped of his bedside lamp then headed back to the living room. All night, my mind had been working hard trying to figure out how I could best help Bryce with the situation with the social worker. I could already tell he was proud and wouldn't accept anything that seemed like an offer of charity.

An idea was forming in my mind of what I might propose, but I didn't know how it would go over. What I did know was that I was determined Liam get to stay with Bryce, and eventually with me.

I couldn't even imagine what it must be like for Liam to worry that he might have to go into the foster system when Bryce was all the family he had left. I knew all too well what it felt like to be abandoned. Even though my adoptive father had been everything a kid could hope for in a parent, and I loved him dearly, it still hurt to know I'd been forsaken by my own parents as a baby.

While the situation wasn't quite the same, Liam and Bryce were dealing with the very real fear they might be separated. It made my heart ache to think about Liam having any of the same abandonment issues I'd worked hard to overcome my entire life, and I'd do anything to shield him from that.

When I came back into the living room, Bryce was leaning back on the couch, his eyes closed. I knew the minute he became aware of my presence by the shift in his body, so subtle I might not have noticed it if I weren't feeling the same thing.

His body tensed slightly and he opened his eyes. We stared at each other for long, drawn out moments. Bryce was the first to tear his gaze away, clearing his throat and sitting up straight.

"Before you tell me it's not needed, I want you to know how much I appreciate, well, everything. The food. What you've done with Liam." He looked back up at me then. "And the support."

I smiled and lowered myself to the couch, so pleased I was helping him even in whatever small ways I had so far. "You're more than welcome. Actually, I wanted to talk to you about something."

This was the perfect opening to put forward my idea. Bryce turned to face me, and I shifted as well, putting myself a little deeper into his personal space. His expression held a mix of curiosity and wariness.

I instinctively wanted to take him in my arms and declare everything would be okay, but we weren't there yet. Maybe, just maybe, if he agreed to what I was about to suggest, things would lead there naturally.

"Liam told me about some of the difficulties with the adoption," I said. His face immediately shuttered, a mask of strength and determination on his features now.

"I'm not going to lose Liam," he stated. "I'll figure this out."

I nodded. "What if I had a solution?"

He cut his gaze to me. "What kind of solution?" The wariness was back, but I didn't let it stop me from putting my idea out there.

"What if there was a way to prove your stability to the state? To show them that Liam had all the assistance he needs—financially and otherwise?"

"What do you mean?"

He had no idea what I was about to propose, and I gathered my resolve to just say it. Knowing in my heart this was the right answer.

"We could...enter into a relationship."

He stared at me. "Meaning…"

I met his gaze, unwavering in my resolve. "Meaning you and me. A relationship. It would show that you have all the financial stability you need for Liam. Also, you'd have support with caring for him. From me. I could help you and him both."

Bryce blinked but otherwise stayed stock-still, obviously shell-shocked. "Why would you do that?"

I bit back the words *because you're my mate and I want to help you*. But I didn't just want to *help* him—I wanted *him*. I was suggesting a solution that might seem crazy to him, but I wanted him to see some of my true intentions as well.

"Bryce," I said, gazing at him, letting some of my desire rise to the surface. "Liam is a talented ball player, and there's no way I'd ever allow him to have to lie awake at night in some foster home and not be able to play ball. To not be with his family. Also…" The corner of my mouth lifted in a smile. "I really like you."

He still didn't seem to understand why I would do this, but I noticed the flare of desire in his eyes in response to my words. He started to shake his head, but I stopped him, reaching up to cup his cheek in my hand.

Fuck. A rush of need coursed through me, every instinct I had demanding I claim this man. I didn't know what he saw on my face, but Bryce sucked in a sharp breath. He drew his lower lip between his teeth, and I nearly lost my grip on my self-control. With as much restraint as I could muster, I drew in a breath of my own, and then forced myself to remain in check.

"Just think about my offer," I said softly. "Besides, I have a feeling we would end up together anyway."

His brow furrowed, but before he could say anything, I brought a finger to his lips. I'd just wanted to tell him to not answer right away but feeling his soft lips against my skin had me slipping. Losing some of that carefully maintained control.

Bryce's eyes were locked on mine, searching and confused, but also raw with want. I didn't think he even realized it when his tongue darted out to nervously lick his lips.

A low growl rumbled in my chest, pure lust overwhelming me, and I had no choice. I couldn't walk away from this man tonight without at least having a taste—and showing him just how good it might be between us if he accepted my offer.

With my hand still on his cheek, I tilted his head higher. A lock of blond hair fell across his forehead, and I brushed it back. Then I leaned in.

Slowly. Surely.

When my lips brushed against his, just a touch, just a tease, it was like the entire earth reverberated. Or maybe it was just my body reacting to his. His breath rushed out in a gasp, warm and sweet, and I breathed in before capturing his lips more fully with mine. Pressing against him. Gently testing, but also determined.

Another growl rumbled deep inside me. Mine.

I lingered there, my lips on his, until his entire body shuddered. When I pulled away, his eyes were darker, his pupils dilated, his breath coming shallow now.

God, I wanted to pull him back into my arms and show him exactly what I was feeling, but I knew I had to be careful. So I made myself stand up and take a step back. It was the hardest thing I'd ever done.

"Think about it," I murmured, giving him one last heated look before I headed to the door as quickly as I could.

Thirty minutes later—as soon as I got home—I went straight to my backyard and shifted. All the pent-up energy inside me had me exploding into wolf form almost as soon as I gave up control to him. He surged out of me and immediately raced into the woods behind my house—which was one of the furthest north in the woods that were our pack territory—getting lost in the depths of the night sounds and scents.

I tried to center myself as my wolf ran, but he was just as elated as I was about finding our fated mate, and my energy twined with my animal's. I really hoped Bryce took me up on my offer because leaving him tonight had been one of the almost painful. I wanted to be with him. I ran, imagining what that might be like, full of hope, but as over the moon as I was, at the back of my mind there was a twinge of worry. Even though we barely knew each other, I was ready to go all in with Bryce. I just knew—felt in my very soul—that it was meant to be, but we had hurdles I didn't know how to overcome yet. First, I had to get Bryce to accept the fact that we were fated. Which meant telling him about shifters. I also had to hope he would feel the same about me the way I was already feeling about him. There was no denying he was attracted to me, but this was all unfamiliar territory, and I wasn't sure how to navigate it.

But as the moon rose higher in the clear night sky, and I continued to run deeper into the woods, I knew I would figure it out. I'd find a way for us to be together—hopefully sooner than later.

Chapter 6 - Bryce

I didn't know how long I sat there, my mind and body reeling from what had just happened. I brushed my fingers over my lips, the nerves raw even though Jaxon had been so gentle. However, with just that simple kiss he'd ignited all kinds of things in me. I'd already been feeling this irresistible draw to Jaxon, but now it was amplified a hundred times.

I smiled, closing my eyes as I recalled every second of the last few minutes with Jaxon. The intensity in his gaze. The determination in his voice when he'd suggested we have a...relationship.

God. That fact was at war for attention in my mind with the lingering sensations in my body as I remembered the feel of his mouth on mine, and how I'd wanted so much more.

I tried to focus on what he'd said. Tried to ignore the rush of desire still pulsing through my veins.

A relationship? I wasn't sure if he meant a real relationship, or some kind of fake relationship to help me adopt Liam, but I couldn't wrap my head around either possibility. Why would Jaxon want to do that? He'd said he wanted to help Liam, but Jaxon also said he thought we could end up together anyway. What did that mean?

I didn't know how to process it all. It was astonishing and worrying at the same time. What were his real motives? Was it all just an effort to help Liam? Even that kiss? I just didn't know. Either way, it was definitely tempting.

The idea of being in a relationship with Jaxon—even if it was fake—held more appeal than I wanted to admit. Jaxon amazed me with the kindness in his heart. It was clear he was truly a good guy, and his offer seemed genuinely selfless. Part of me felt it would be completely wrong to take advantage of him, whatever his intentions may be, but I had more than myself to think of here. At the end of the day, this came back to Liam, and I'd do anything in my power to keep Liam. He was all I had left.

The idea Jaxon proposed made sense when I looked at it that way. I was still confused, though. Pushing up from the couch, I grabbed my cane and made my way to the bedroom. It wasn't like I had to figure all this out tonight. It had been a long day, and I needed some rest.

But as I made my way through the room, I picked up on a scent lingering in the air. I'd noticed it before. It was unusual, but in a good way. In fact, the scent seemed to make my desire climb even higher. That's when I realized the scent was Jaxon's, and that every time he was around I experienced the same wild longing I was feeling now.

I inhaled deeply, and immediately felt a warm pull, low in my belly. Recalling Jaxon's kiss, my dick twitched to life, and I barely suppressed a moan as my body began to hum with need. God, what was he doing to me? My desire reached shocking levels until I was hard and wanting to be fucked so bad. Then slick suddenly coated my ass, and I knew. I quickly calculated days in my head, and then groaned aloud. I hadn't been able to afford to get my prescription filled for my heat suppressors last time, and if my calculations were correct, it was due.

Great. On top of everything else I was dealing with, I was going into heat. Just what I needed.

***

"Eat your cereal," I told Liam from across the kitchen where I was trying to stay busy cleaning up.

Liam had been talking non-stop all morning about practice and how awesome Jaxon was. I was thrilled for him, but every mention of Jaxon's name had my heat spiking higher.

I was doing everything I could to not let it show to Liam—hence the furious scrubbing of the frying pan—but I couldn't remember ever having a heat this intense before.

I needed him to finish up his breakfast so I could get him off to school and get back home before things really got out of control.

"Will you be there next weekend, Uncle Bryce?"

"I'm sorry, what?" I'd completely missed his question, his last mention of Jaxon sending me back to relive our kiss last night. My skin felt hot, sweat beading on the back of my neck, and my slick was ridiculously distracting. As was the throbbing need in my pants. Jesus. I had to get this under control.

"I asked if you'll be able to come to our first game next weekend. You know, with your pain and all..." Liam looked at me with both hope and concern in his eyes.

"Of course I'll be there, big man! You know I wouldn't miss that for the world. I'll be there, no matter what kind of pain I might be in. I can't wait."

He grinned, then hopped up from the table and put his dishes in the dishwasher. "Me either."

We headed out to the car, and as I pulled out of the drive, Liam surprised me with the heavy change of subject. "I'm worried about what Mrs. Pinder said."

My heart sank. "Liam, I don't want you to worry about that. All you need to know is that you'll be with me, no matter what."

"She said it might be a hard battle." His frown deepened.

It made me so angry that Mrs. Pinder said that in front of him. She talked about having his best interests at heart, but she seemed to really be missing basics of what was important.

"Liam, listen to me," I said firmly. "I will do everything in my power to adopt you. It's happening. No matter what. So I don't want you spend another minute worrying about it."

He gave me a tentatively hopeful smile. "Jaxon said—" The way his eyes lit up in adoration every time he mentioned Jaxon had my heart doing all kinds of crazy things. Thinking of him yet again had my body responding in kind, a sense of longing like I'd never known filling me. "He said the same thing. He said he would make sure of it."

Jaxon had told him that? I nodded slowly, not wanting to say the wrong thing, but wanting to put Liam's mind at ease before he started his school day.

"Actually, Jaxon mentioned something to me about that too. He wants to help ensure that I'll definitely be able to adopt you."

A smile broke over Liam's face, like the sun on a cloudy day, and I wondered if there would be any way I could say no to Jaxon's offer when it put that look on Liam's face.

"Jaxon is the best, isn't he? I can't believe he's my coach. And that he's hanging out with us. Isn't it just too cool?"

I chuckled at his enthusiasm, but I didn't disagree. It was all so much to take in. That someone like Jaxon Parsons would take an interest in us—in me. I couldn't expect him to truly want someone like me—someone poor and disabled who came with so much baggage, so I had to remind myself that, despite whatever I was feeling for him, it was all for Liam's sake.

We pulled up to the school, which was actually close enough that Liam could walk, but I couldn't, so we drove because I wanted to make sure he got safely inside the school, to see with my own eyes he was okay.

"You know what I wish?" Liam asked, turning to me, whispering like he was revealing a deep secret. "I wish you would ask Jaxon to be your boyfriend."

I huffed out a surprised laugh, but Liam just gave me a look.

"I can tell that you like him." He grinned shyly, just a hint of mischief gleaming in his eyes.

I knew he hadn't connected the dots with what little I'd said. There was no way he had any idea that Jaxon was basically proposing just that.

"Liam," I said, thinking I should say something to him. I didn't need him getting ideas when I wasn't even sure what to do about Jaxon's offer, but I realized now wasn't a good time to hash things out.

He looked at me and quirked an eyebrow that reminded me so much of his mom. "Yes, Uncle Bryce?"

I smiled, then reached out and squeezed his hand. "Have a great day at school, okay, big man?"

"Will do!" he said, hopping out of the car before turning to shout to one of his friends and then darting off across the school yard.

I chuckled, then circled back around the school lot and headed back home. The whole way there I thought about what Liam had said. That he could tell I liked Jaxon, and that he wanted him to be my boyfriend. Liam wasn't wrong. I did like Jaxon, and a huge part of me wondered what it would be like to be with him.

The idea filled my thoughts as I made my way inside my house and finished cleaning up from breakfast. Jaxon in my house. Spending time together. Sharing those looks. Sharing more kisses. I let myself fall deeper into my fantasy, imagining him in my bed. His hands on my body. My mouth on his.

I groaned as my heat somehow kicked in even stronger. Blowing out a breath, I swiped my arm over my forehead then raked my hands through my hair. My body felt like it was on fire. My blood was simmering just beneath the surface, my skin flushed and damp with sweat.

Fuck, I'd never experienced a heat like this. This wasn't just full-blown heat, this was an all-consuming, overpowering need I didn't quite understand.

Finishing up the dishes, I tried to focus on something else. Anything else besides this throbbing ache inside me and the warm slick that seemed to be never ending. I ground my teeth together, and then began pacing the room, trying to exert some of the energy racing through me, trying to release some of the adrenaline that was making me feel like I might come right out of my skin.

When I pressed my palm hard against my cock, hoping to relieve some of the pressure, it only made things worse. I whimpered, white-hot need consuming me. I could only think of one other thing that might help.

As soon as the thought hit me, I was already unzipping my pants and pulling my cock out. I wrapped my hand around it and exhaled with a massive groan. Bracing my other hand against the wall, I began to stroke myself.

Just like the other night, images of Jaxon floated in my mind, and my climax began to build almost instantly. Only this time, I had real a life experience to add to my fantasy; and the memory of Jaxon's full lips on mine sent shudders through my body.

I came hard and fast, crying out his name. I stood there for a few moments, trying to catch my breath and process how that might well have been the best orgasm of my life—and how if that was just from my own fantasies, what it might be like to actually come with Jaxon's body pressed against mine. Buried deep inside me.

I groaned, realizing this hadn't even taken the edge off. Instead, those thoughts make my heat impossibly stronger. The only thing I could think about in that moment was that I wanted to take Jaxon up on his offer—true intentions be damned.

Chapter 7 - Jaxon

It was mid-afternoon when I walked into the lodge to visit my father. We hadn't talked about me taking over the pack since our first conversation last week, and I knew he'd want to know where I stood on that, but I'd come for another reason today.

"Jaxon." Dad greeted me with a warm smile as I stood in the doorway of his office. He pushed back from his desk and came around it to give me a hug. "To what do I owe this surprise visit?" His eyes lit up. "Have you been thinking any more about becoming pack leader?"

I smiled. "It's been on my mind, for sure, but that's not what I wanted to talk to you about."

"Come. Sit down." He led me over to the sitting area this time. "What's going on?"

My smile widened. "I've found my fated mate."

My father sat back, his own smile spreading. "That's wonderful, Jax. Who is it?"

I chuckled. "Well, no one you know, actually."

His brow furrowed. He knew everyone in the pack and most of the shifters in the area. Then it hit him. "A human?"

I nodded, then sighed. "Yeah."

"When did this happen?"

"Last week. The day I talked to you, actually."

My father chuckled. "Right after you were telling me you weren't sure you could be the alpha if you hadn't found your mate? Funny how fate works."

"Yes, but..." I knew he wouldn't like what I had to say next. "I'm still not sure I'm ready, Dad."

His excitement over me finding my mate faded slightly. "Why not? Jaxon, surely you see how you were made for this. Everyone else sees it."

Yeah, everyone else didn't see what I struggled with internally either. They only saw the front I put on. I scrubbed a hand over my jaw. "I just don't know that I have what it takes to lead the whole pack. I don't want to let anyone down."

Especially him. I couldn't take it if I failed my father in something as big as this.

He sighed. "Look, I'm not going to say I'm not disappointed. I'd hoped you'd see right away that you're the right choice, but I get it. It's a big step. Take all the time you need, Jaxon."

"Thank you. Seriously," I said. I definitely needed more time to process everything, especially in light of what had developed with me finding my mate.

"So tell me more about this mate," he said, shifting the topic as if he could read my mind.

My shoulders relaxed slightly, my grin returning as I thought of Bryce. "His name is Bryce. I met him at Kay's Diner last week. He has a kid."

My father's eyebrows rose, but he didn't say anything, no doubt wanting to hear more.

"Well, it's not his kid. He's raising his nephew. His sister died last year, and he's working to gain custody of Liam."

"How old is Liam?"

"Eight. He's playing ball on my team, actually. He's good friends with Cole."

Dad smiled. "You sound fond of him."

"Yeah," I said. "He's remarkable. A great ball player, and an even more amazing kid. You'll like him."

"When can I meet them?"

"Well, that's the thing…" I tried to gather my thoughts. "They're both human, and have no idea the shifter world even exists, much less the concept of fated mates."

"Ah," he said, nodding. "Yes, that's often a concern when a shifter finds a human mate, but nothing I'd worry too much about, son."

"There's more. Bryce is…struggling. He's raising his nephew alone and going for custody. But the state seems to be giving him trouble about it. Needing to make sure he's capable of supporting him."

My dad frowned. "And why's that?"

"Well, Bryce was injured. I'm not sure of the details, but I'm guessing it might have something to do with what happened to his sister. Just a hunch. However, it left him disabled, and apparently money has been tight. Both Bryce and Liam are worried about the adoption going through."

"Sounds like they need you."

I nodded, leaning forward and bracing my elbows on my knees. "They do. And I…have a plan. That's what I wanted to talk to you about."

"You know you can ask me anything."

I did. My dad had always been there for me, a strong force that provided stability. To me and the rest of the pack. It was no wonder I felt like I had such big shoes to fill.

"I want to help Bryce with the adoption by helping provide some of the support he needs. Financially and otherwise. It's a lot on him to take care of Liam all alone."

I went on to tell him about the plan I'd come up with to declare a relationship with Bryce. How I thought that would help with the adoption case, proving that Bryce had everything he needed to take care of Liam.

"Why don't you bring them up here? Move them in with you on the property. Having them on shifter territory would give them all the support they need."

I nodded. "I thought of that, and honestly, that's my preferred option, but I don't think it's the best idea. Not yet. They don't know anything about shifters, and it might just all be too much too soon."

I could tell by the way he looked at me that he could sense my underlying concern about them finding out.

"I see your point. But I wouldn't overly worry about that, Jaxon. If he's your mate, it will all work out."

That's what I kept telling myself, and it felt good to have my dad confirm it, but it didn't erase all my concerns.

"I think it would be best to wait to tell them, though. At least until I can make Bryce fall in love with me. Then I can claim him as my mate."

He furrowed his brows. "I have no doubt he'll fall in love with you. But don't wait too long, son. You don't want to start a relationship off on the wrong foot by keeping secrets, and it's dangerous enough you're going into a relationship with the adoption issue over your head."

"I know, but I don't want to mess this up."

The truth of it was, despite the fact that Bryce was my mate and I knew without a doubt we were meant to be together, I couldn't help but worry about how he'd react when he found out about me being a shifter. Some humans never really accepted the concept, and the fact that Bryce might reject me, seriously set my nerves on edge.

Just then, my phone buzzed. I pulled it from my back pocket, my heart leaping when I saw there was a text from Bryce.

If not, that's fine. I'll sort it out.

I frowned. What did that mean? Then I saw the text directly above it. One I'd missed somehow.

Would you be able to pick Liam up for practice tonight?

Shit. That one had been sent over an hour ago. How had I missed it?

"Dad, I have to go. I'm sorry. I scheduled an extra practice this evening at the last minute, since our first game is coming up soon. I need to pick up Liam on the way."

"Yeah, absolutely," he said, standing. I stood as well and gave him a quick hug. Before I could rush out the door though, he caught my shoulder. "Jaxon, I'm really happy for you that you've found your mate. I know it will all be fine. And I can't wait to meet Bryce and Liam."

I grinned. "I can't wait either."

Then I rushed out of the lodge and hopped in my car, excitement filling me as I knew I was about to see my mate again. Maybe the night might end up where we left off.

***

Unfortunately, as I headed toward Bryce's place I realized I wasn't going to have time to pick Liam up and get to the ball field before the kids and parents started arriving. A little upset, I ended up asking Linc to collect Liam, hoping Bryce didn't think I was trying to avoid him. That was the last thing I wanted him to think.

Practice went well, though. All the kids were excited about our upcoming game next weekend, Liam most of all. His enthusiasm was contagious, and halfway through practice, the team was on a roll. I couldn't wait for the first game.

As we wrapped things up, I called Liam over. "Hey, buddy, what do you say that instead of going out to eat, we swing by the grocery store and I cook something for you and Bryce?"

"Seriously?" he asked, grinning so wide I couldn't help but laugh.

"Seriously. You can help me pick out some stuff you like too."

"Ice cream," he said without missing a beat. "We only get ice cream on special occasions." He bit his lip. "I mean, if that's okay…"

I felt a pang in my heart, realizing how much Bryce was sacrificing to provide for Liam, and how hard it really must be on them, but there was something I could do about that.

"I think this amazing practice is special occasion enough. We'll load up on ice cream," I said with a wink.

He beamed at me, then helped me finish loading up equipment, stopping every few minutes to say goodbye to his teammates. When we got to the grocery store, I gave him free rein, telling him to pick out anything he wanted.

The mix of shock and delight he rewarded me with was enough to melt my heart. I made sure to get plenty of healthy food, but Liam deserved to enjoy some treats. By the time we finished up at the store, the cart was full and the sun was starting to set.

"We better get moving," I told Liam as we loaded up my car. "Your uncle will wonder what's taking so long."

Liam talked my ear off the entire ride back to his house, enthusing about practice and speculating about the team we'd be up against for our first game. I just laughed and let him talk, but as we pulled up in front of his house, my mind was firmly on Bryce.

Nervous energy skittered through me as I wondered what things would be like tonight, especially with that kiss still lingering between us.

Gathering up as many grocery bags as I could, I followed Liam into the house—and nearly dropped everything I was holding.

It hit me like a freight train. The scent filling the air. It was undeniable. My omega was in heat.

"Jaxon," Bryce croaked, shock all over his face. He was standing in the middle of the living room in nothing but a pair of sweatpants.

I dug my fingers into the grocery bags hard enough to tear into the paper. And it took everything I had in me not to toss them to the ground and rush over and take him in my arms.

He swallowed hard, and I could hear him even from across the room. Every one of my senses seemed to be jacked up to full throttle. The rhythmic pumping of his heart, speeding up as he locked eyes with me. The unnatural warmth of the room, so hot that Bryce was sweating. The scent of him emanating stronger with every thud of his pulse.

Fuck.

"We got groceries, Uncle Bryce," Liam exclaimed, darting through the room and into the kitchen beyond.

The knowledge that he was there was pretty much the only thing keeping me under control. I tried to keep my features calm, but inside I felt like I was losing my mind. My wolf reared up, urging me to claim my mate right fucking now.

"I didn't think you'd be stopping by," Bryce said, his voice thick. His eyes were nearly black, dark with desire.

Christ.

I stared at him. His shoulders were broad, his arms toned. His torso was long and lean, chiseled, but not overly so, tapering down to narrow hips. My gaze dropped further, taking in the bulge in his pants.

Holy fucking hell.

My cock sprang to attention, hard and ready to go in a second flat. Need pulsed through me. Hot lust that demanded I take action. Clearing my throat, I dragged my gaze back to his. He also looked like he was barely restraining himself. His eyes were fevered, his skin flushed. God, I'd had no idea being near an omega in heat—not just any omega, but my mate—was so overpowering.

"I was running behind earlier," I managed to say, explaining why I hadn't been the one to pick up Liam before practice. But god, if I had been, I was pretty sure I never would have made it out of this house. "I thought I'd make dinner for you guys."

I took a step forward. Just one, but the air around us thickened even with that slight narrowing of space. We stared at each other, so much unspoken desire radiating between us, but the moment was broken when Liam raced back through the room.

"I'll grab the rest!"

I blew out a breath and forced myself to move toward the kitchen. Doing so, however, required me to step around Bryce. My arm brushed against his as I did, and I felt as if I'd been burned. His skin was blazing. He jerked his head to look at me, a gasp on his lips. The fact that he was obviously feeling this too sent my own need climbing higher.

Dinner. Right.

I kept moving into the kitchen, setting the bags on the counter before I started unloading them. Liam rushed back in and began helping, already diving in to tell Bryce about practice.

Somehow, I managed to focus on the task at hand—putting away the groceries—but I kept darting glances at Bryce. Every time, I found him staring right back at me. When I finished putting things away with Liam's help, I turned to Bryce.

"Steak sound good?"

He nodded, pushing forward with his cane, the muscle in his jaw ticking. He closed the distance between us, and I swear I got impossibly harder. His scent hit me again—oh god, I could smell his slick—as he came up next to me and lifted his hand.

He reached behind my head and opened a cabinet, and I had to grip the edge of the counter to keep my hands to myself. Fuck I wanted to touch him, and his chest was just inches from me. He grabbed a pan and handed it to me but didn't let go as I took it. My fingers brushed against his, and I saw his body stiffen, every muscle frozen. He watched me, questions in his eyes.

I let my gaze drop to his chest again, and a fresh wave of heat poured off him. When I met his eyes once more, I managed to lift my lips in a smile, letting him know I was aware of how he was feeling and that I fully intended to do something about it.

"Later," I murmured with a wink.

He sucked in a breath, and I chuckled. At least I wasn't suffering alone.

I got to work making dinner, telling Bryce to take it easy. He disappeared for a moment, and then came back, now wearing a shirt. I wanted to protest, but I guessed it would seem a little odd if he sat down to dinner naked from the waist up. Still, I missed the seeing all that flesh, and I let Bryce know, even if was only none verbal.

Liam was a good little sous chef, and I kept him busy enough that he didn't seem to notice the heated looks passing between Bryce and me.

By the time dinner was done, Bryce was shifting restlessly in the chair he'd taken at the kitchen table. His knee bounced up and down, and his knuckles were white where he gripped them together. It was obvious he was trying desperately to hold back how much he was affected by my presence right now. He looked like he didn't quite understand the intensity of what was happening. His heat would be amplified in my presence, I knew that much. The draw of an omega in heat to his fated mate was one of the most powerful urges in existent. There was no containing it. He was doing a damn good job trying, though. Liam seemed completely oblivious.

We managed to make it through the meal, but Liam was already yawning when he started clearing the dishes.

"Why don't you let me take care of these?" I pushed back from my chair. "I'll get you off to bed."

Liam jumped at the offer and darted out of the room saying he just had to brush his teeth.

That left Bryce and I alone again for the first time since I'd walked in. I stood there for a moment, staring down at him. His breath hitched as I came around the table to stand next to him.

"I'll be back in ten minutes," I told him, my voice low and full of promise. My wolf howled inside me, raging that I was this close to my mate and not doing a damn thing about it yet. I knew there would be no resisting this once Liam was off to sleep.

I left Bryce sitting there staring after me, wondering what he was thinking. Wondering how he would react when it was just the two of us. No distractions. Nothing except our desire between us. For that matter, I wasn't quite sure how I'd react. What I was certain of, though, was there was no escaping the need to do *something*.

When I got to Liam's room, he was already climbing into bed and pulling his blankets up around him. "This was the best day ever! First practice, then you cooked dinner for us."

I chuckled, sitting down on the edge of the bed. "I'm glad you had fun."

"I wish we could do this every day," he said, surprising me.

"What do you mean?"

"If you could be with us every day. Maybe even live here with me and Bryce!"

My eyes widened, shocked he'd want that so much, but it was also what I wanted. "You know, I'd like that too. In fact, I'm working on something along those lines right now."

Liam grinned, almost knowingly, and it made me wonder if he'd seen or heard anything from Bryce that would have him thinking like that. God, I hoped so. I told Liam goodnight and turned off his lamp, then shut his door behind me. Without waiting another second, I strode toward the kitchen. Bryce was still there, but now he was standing by the kitchen counter, wiping a bead of sweat from his brow.

He turned toward me, going still, and I stopped right before I reached him, leaving only three feet between us.

Uncertainty warred with hunger. It was written all over him, in the way he looked at me, the way he held his body. Like he was barely restraining from flinging himself into my arms.

"Jaxon," he whispered, his voice thick and full of longing. "I don't..."

I looked at him, making sure he saw every bit of desire I was feeling. "I do. I want this, Bryce. I want you."

The attraction connecting us was undeniable. The pull irresistible. With him in heat, and my obvious reaction to him, there was no holding back. Bryce seemed to let go of everything he'd been holding onto, closing the distance between us in three quick steps, his limp barely slowing him down.

The minute his body crashed into mine, I lost my control. Grabbing his head with both hands, I jerked it up toward mine and crushed my mouth to his.

A strangled moan escaped his lips, and I delved inside the second they parted. Backing him up against the counter, I plundered his mouth, ravished him. Took everything I wanted in a searing, demanding kiss.

The taste of him hit my tongue, exploding in fire that raced through my body. Bryce's hips rocked forward, the bulge of his cock grinding against mine, and a growl rumbled through my chest. He dug his fingers into my shirt, and I released my grip on him only long enough to reach behind me and yank it over my head. Seconds later, I tore his off as well.

Then we were skin to skin, and I barely managed not to take him where we stood. Without another word, I scooped him up in my arms and strode back through the house. Straight to his bedroom.

Chapter 8 - Bryce

Oh my god, YES!

I clung to Jaxon's shoulders, my body humming with anticipation. Unbridled lust coursed through me, passion like I'd never known rising up inside. Fuck me. There was no mistaking it, Jaxon was igniting things I'd never imagined. My heat was more intense than anything I'd ever felt before.

I could barely think straight as Jaxon carried me into my room and laid me down on my bed. Staring up at him, my body screamed for me to reach out and pull him to me, to feel his mouth pressed against mine again, but somewhere in the depths of my mind a tiny alarm sounded.

This was dangerous. My heat was out of control, making both Jaxon and I react in ways we might not otherwise. Except having him here on my bed, his green eyes molten as he moved toward me again, made me think that maybe I would, even if I weren't in heat. I wanted to experience everything this man had to offer.

But there was too much at stake.

"Jaxon." I placed a hand on his chest to stop him from moving closer. The feel of his skin beneath my fingers nearly had me forgetting what I needed to say.

But he paused, his brow creasing as he studied me. "Bryce?"

I steeled myself to say the words. "I don't think this is a good idea."

His gaze roved over my face. Down my chest. Landing on my throbbing cock, which twitched as a result. "Are you sure about that?"

No. Not at all.

"I just…" Fuck, this was awkward. "I just don't want this to be a mistake."

He shook his head. "This is the furthest thing from a mistake." But he must have seen my concerns written all over my face because he sat back on his heels and blew out a hard breath. The tension on his features made it clear he was barely holding back.

"This isn't just about sex, Bryce."

Was it not?

"It's so much more than that," he said, continuing. "I really like you, and that has nothing to do with anything except you being you." Jaxon reached out and ran a finger down my chest, causing the muscles to tighten while injecting a fresh flare of desire deep in my belly. "I want a relationship with you. I want *you*."

I tried to believe that. I really wanted to believe that, but how could that be possible? This had to be my heat making him say these things, right? I thought he meant what he was saying—in this moment, but how would he feel tomorrow or the next day?

Jaxon leaned in slowly, his gaze on mine as his lips claimed me again. Softer this time. Testing. When his tongue brushed out to trace the seam of my lips, I moaned, my body bucking up against his. He smiled against my mouth, then deepened the kiss. Not rushing me, not pressuring me, simply taking his time, and in that moment I lost all my resistance. I needed this. Needed him.

I'd dealt with too much pain and stress for too long now, all my worries and fears that had plagued me lately only compounding the physical aches in my body. I needed a release. To let go, even for just one night. To simply enjoy the moment for once in my life.

I felt the shift between us the moment I returned his kiss, giving in. As if he recognized that surrender, a growl rumbled deep in his chest and he captured my face in his hands, tilting it up so he could kiss me even more thoroughly.

"Yes, fuck, Jaxon," I groaned when he ran one hand down my neck, scraping his fingers along my sensitive flesh.

It was like he snapped, unleashing all the pent-up desire he'd been holding back. I could sense the alpha in him rising to the surface, his recognition of an omega in heat. I knew there was no stopping an alpha in rut.

And I knew now I didn't want to.

Gone were the slow kisses. Jaxon kept his mouth on mine as he trailed his hand lower, and I kissed him back with all the want and longing I had in me. I slid my hands around his strong shoulders, digging my fingers in hard, a cry of pleasure escaping my mouth when he made contact with my aching cock, even just through my sweats. I ground my hips against his, the pain for once subsiding, challenged by the pure pleasure racing along every limb.

Jaxon yanked at the waistband of my pants, expertly ridding me of them without breaking our kiss. I skimmed my hands down his sides to his narrow waist, then fumbled with his zipper. God, if I didn't feel him now, I thought I might die.

Jaxon chuckled against my mouth, then pulled away, raising up on his knees as he rested his hands on the button of his jeans. I squirmed beneath him, trapped between his thighs.

With his gaze boring into mine, he slowly unfastened his jeans, then slid the zipper down. My breath caught as he reached for his cock. His jaw clenched, and I swallowed hard. When he pulled his cock out, another flood of my heat coursed through me. Pheromones filled the air and my slick flowed.

"Fuck, Bryce," he said, his pupils nearly black. "Do you have any idea how fucking sexy you are?"

I whimpered in need at his words, then found myself responding in a way I never would have thought. A little bit taunting. A little bit cocky. Way surer of myself than I expected.

"Why don't you show me?"

A wicked grin tilted his lips, and I felt my body shudder. He was the one who was too sexy for words. I'd never seen a man's body that was so perfect. Not in real life. So perfectly sculpted, all hard lines and angles.

He reached for my hand and wrapped it around his cock, and I squeezed hard. Holy shit. He was big. So thick, so long. My ass clenched around emptiness, and I knew I needed him inside me, like...yesterday.

Precum beaded on the wide tip, and I ran my thumb over it, drawing a groan from Jaxon. I smiled, loving that I was making him feel this way. Making him lose control. But Jaxon wasn't one to give up control easily. Reaching between us, he stroked a finger between my ass cheeks, his eyes going darker still when he realized how slick I was.

I stroked him harder, loving the grunts I was drawing from him, but I was the one mumbling incoherently when he pressed the tip of his finger inside my hole.

"Oh, god," I moaned. "Yes!"

"You like that?" He pressed in further before slowly pulling back out, running his finger along my clenching walls. I pushed against him, needing him back inside me, and he let out a low chuckle.

He traced circles around my bud, gathering my slick and rubbing it all over my hole, and my entire body convulsed. Then he pushed back inside, harder this time, deeper.

I squeezed my eyes shut and bit my lip, lost in the feel of Jaxon's cock throbbing in my hand and his finger fucking my ass. He moved in and out of me, adding another finger. When he scissored them, I gripped his cock tighter, and he groaned again.

Then he was pulling out of me, taking my hands and pinning them above my head. He lowered his mouth to mine again, rougher this time. Need and desperation seeping through. I met him stroke for stroke, teeth and tongues and lips colliding as we nearly devoured each other.

My body was on fire, hot and desperate, begging for more. My ass clenched again, and when Jaxon pulled back this time, his face was drawn tight with restraint again. He moved to position his cock at my entrance, teasing my hole with his cockhead.

He glanced at me uncertainly, as if he wanted to be sure I wanted this as much as he did.

"Please." It was all I said before he was slamming inside me, filling me completely. His thick cock stretched me as he drove in deep, bottoming out. I cried out. However, the unexpected shock at being filled so quickly was replaced almost immediately with an overwhelming sense of pleasure that had my mind and body reeling.

Jaxon stilled, his eyes on mine, concern in his gaze, almost as if he was afraid he'd hurt me. And that's when I realized—that's exactly what it was. He didn't want to hurt me. He was looking at me so tenderly, I felt my heart rate speed up for entirely other reasons than the fact it had never felt this good to have a man inside me like it did right now.

"Are you okay?" he asked softly.

Reaching for him, I scraped my fingers down his torso then gripped his hips, pulling them hard against me.

"More," I said in answer, and a smile flitted across his face.

Then he was gripping the back of my knees, pushing them toward my chest, angling his hips until he was even deeper. When he slammed inside me again, harder this time, my mind spun, all rational thought fleeing.

Somewhere in the recesses of my lust-filled brain, I remembered I didn't have any condoms in the house—it wasn't like I ever thought I'd be having sex—but when I looked up at Jaxon and saw the nearly feral expression on his face, the thought slipped away and I lost myself to the moment.

A million sensations hit me at once as he began to move, finding a rhythm that drove me insane. The scent of my slick and his masculine musk mingled together. Sweat beaded on his brow as he pounded into me over and over again. And the sound of his voice as he growled my name. The look of ecstasy on his face... Oh god.

I felt a tingling at the base of my spine, and my balls tightened. Jaxon was about to send me right over the edge. My internal walls clenched and convulsed around him, and he grunted, his eyes rolling back in his head.

Then I felt the strangest thing. The base of Jaxon's cock, buried deep inside my ass, seemed to swell impossibly larger. Thicker. Fuller. Like I tight ball was forming, locking him inside of me. I didn't understand what was happening, but I knew that the most intense pleasure I'd ever known began to radiate through me. Starting deep inside where Jaxon was buried, then shooting out through my entire body.

White-hot heat seared my veins, and it felt as if electric sparks were igniting in every nerve ending. Then I was coming, thick jets shooting from my cock as Jaxon continued to claim my body, almost primally.

I cried out, his name falling from my lips. He opened his eyes, locking that gaze on me, and he looked more than primal in that moment. Raw. Uninhibited. Nearly savage.

He leaned over me and crushed his mouth to mine just as his own orgasm took hold of him. I dug my fingers into his back, clutching him to me as his body shuddered. My release was still erupting from me, my body convulsing with the sheer force of it.

I'd never come this hard before—ever, and that included the last two times I'd masturbated thinking of Jaxon. I didn't know what to make of it. All I could do was surrender myself to the marvel of what he was doing to me.

When Jaxon cried out my name with one last thrust, I swallowed his moans in a passionate kiss, pouring everything I was feeling into it.

Out of breath and spent, Jaxon carefully rolled off me, taking me with him, but his cock stayed firmly lodged inside me. We laid on our sides, facing each other, gasping for air. I could barely process what had just happened. I only knew I'd never felt this good.

After a few minutes, Jaxon finally pulled out, his cock still hard, but there was no sign of the odd swelling I'd felt before. I was about to ask him about it, but he stood from the bed and leaned down to brush the hair from my face.

"I'm going to run a bath," he said with a smile. "Don't go anywhere."

I huffed out a breathless laugh as he turned and headed toward the bathroom. Like I could go anywhere even if I wanted to. My body felt like a limp noodle, totally relaxed, but funnily enough I also felt more energized than I had in a long time. As if all the tension I'd been feeling for so long had depleted.

God, I'd needed that more than I realized.

Jaxon came back into the bedroom and reached for me. I started to stand up, but he shook his head and leaned down, cradling me in his arms as if I weighed nothing.

"I've got you."

I rested my head on his chest, letting him carry me. He set me down gently in the steaming bathtub then kneeled beside me. Taking a cloth from the side of the tub, he dipped it in the water, then began wringing it out over me. The trickles of hot water on my skin relaxed me even more, and I found myself allowing Jaxon to take care of me like this. Enjoying it even.

He pampered me, gently washing every part of my body. When he tilted my head back to rest on the edge of the bathtub and started massaging shampoo into my hair, I sighed.

Jaxon chuckled softly. "How do you feel?"

"So fucking good," I moaned, then realized what I'd sounded like. My gaze darted to his, but I just found him watching me with a small smile on his face.

"Good."

I thought again about what we'd done, and how it had felt like nothing I'd ever experienced in my life, and I furrowed my brows. "Jaxon…" How was I supposed to say this? But I had to know.

He arched a brow. "Everything okay?"

"I just—well..." I cleared my throat and tried again. "When you were...inside me." God, I hoped he didn't see the blush I felt creeping over me. The moment had passed, and I wasn't sure if I should feel awkward now I'd had heat-induced sex with a man I barely knew.

"When I was fucking you?" he asked, his voice lower, full of heat again.

"Yeah," I said with a small laugh. "That. Well, I felt you, I don't know, swell or something. Almost like there was a bulge at the base of your—like you were..." Shit. I don't know. It sounded ridiculous to say it out loud.

But Jaxon didn't seem surprised or confused. Instead, he looked almost wary. He cleared his throat. "Yeah. That can happen sometimes." He looked at me more sharply now, his eyes serious. "It's because we're fated mates."

What? He'd lost me there.

"What do you mean?"

Jaxon took a minute to answer, and I didn't miss the way his jaw ticked. He rinsed the shampoo from my hair before speaking.

"It just means that sometimes people are meant to be together. You know, fate and all that." But it sounded like there was much more to it than that.

"And you think we're..."

"Mates. Yep."

Jaxon had previously said he thought we were meant to be together. Did he really think that? It seemed impossible. I felt overwhelmed, confused. Worst of all, hopeful. But I couldn't let myself get wrapped up in the idea that Jaxon and I could actually have a real relationship. I had to keep my head on straight. Even though it was clear how easily Jaxon could make me lose it.

I force a laugh. "Don't get your hopes up there," I said, trying to keep my voice light. Like what I was saying didn't make me feel raw and vulnerable. "There's no way someone like you would ever be fated to someone like me."

Jaxon stopped and met my eyes this time. "Why would you say something like that?"

"Well, I mean...look at me."

His eyes heated. "I am, and I'm telling you I don't want to hear anything like that. I want a relationship with you, Bryce, remember?"

I swallowed. He sounded so serious about it, but it didn't make sense. "Yeah, to help Liam. I get that, and I honestly appreciate it, but what just happened between us doesn't mean you have to feel obligated to either of us in any way."

Jaxon scoffed, an incredulous look on his gorgeous face. "Believe me, I don't feel obligated. I want this. I'm not sure how to get you to understand that, but just trust me here. Please." He frowned, as if he was considering saying more, then nodded like he decided to go with it. "In fact, I'd really like us to move in together."

I was apparently in for shock after shock tonight. I instantly wanted to leap at the idea—for more reasons than just Liam's adoption. The idea of being with this man night after night—possibly in my bed—held a massive amount of appeal.

Be careful.

That little voice had me crushing all and any hope that just kept popping up because no matter what happened here, I didn't truly believe Jaxon wanted a real relationship. Was it worth the potential heartache to go along with his plan?

"Isn't that a bit much so soon?" I asked, my voice strained because I was fairly sure I could fall for this man in a heartbeat.

Jaxon blew out a breath, some of the tension that had cropped up leaving along with it. "Just think about it, okay? I really think it could help with the case."

Right. The case. Yeah, it would serve me well to keep that at the forefront of my mind.

Jaxon helped me out of the bath before wrapping me in a robe. Then he led me back to the bedroom. He turned back the covers and fluffed my pillows then took my hand and drew me to the bed. I eased down, and he was overly attentive to helping me get settled. His gentleness made my heart thump a little harder. Strangely, though, I didn't feel any of the stiffness in my back or hips, which was my constant companion.

I could have gotten myself from the bathroom into the bed just fine on my own, maybe not even needing my cane the way I was feeling, but I also kind of liked how sweet and attentive he was being, so I let him fuss over me. When I was all settled, he came around to the other side of the bed and climbed in, shocking me again. I was starting to lose count.

He pulled me to him, wrapping his arm around my waist and pressing a kiss to my shoulder. I'd thought he might leave, but it looked like he was sticking around.

"Do you want to stay the night?" I blurted out the question before I could think better of it.

He smiled then chuckled. "I thought you'd never ask."

***

Light pricked my eyelids, waking me up from the most peaceful sleep I'd had in longer than I could remember. I felt amazing. Then it all came back to me in a rush, and my eyes flew open. Jaxon.

We'd fallen asleep here in my bed last night after... Oh god. I sat up, looking around the room. The curtains were open—there was the reason I'd woken up—we'd never gotten around to closing them last night, but I didn't see Jaxon. The clock on the nightstand showed it was still early, a good thirty minutes before my alarm was set to go off.

I threw the covers off and scrambled from my bed before grabbing my cane. Had he left sometime during the night? As I made my way into the hall, I noticed Liam's door was wide open, but there was no sign of him inside.

I felt a prickle at the back of my neck, a shiver running through me. "Liam?" No answer. I limped over to his door and looked closer. Yeah, he wasn't in there. I called his name again as I made my way into the kitchen and living room, faster than I should have been able to, and more or less without pain.

It was still there, lingering in the depths of my muscles and bones, but it was overshadowed by the concern for my nephew. That's when I noticed a note taped to the front door. Plucking it off, I read the same scrawled handwriting I'd seen on the napkin Jaxon gave Liam the first night we met.

Took Liam out for breakfast and dropping him off at school. But I'm coming back immediately after.

-J

I leaned against the door, relieved, and also a little flustered. Of course he'd taken care of Liam. That was his M.O. it seemed, but he was coming back here. Where we'd be alone. Again.

For the first time, I realized my heat had subsided. It might flare up later unless I had sex again, but for now it seemed Jaxon had attended thoroughly to that problem as well. My body still felt flushed at the idea of him coming back here, though.

I walked back to the living room, noticing again how my body didn't feel as tight as it normally did. God, that had been the most amazing sex of my life. I'd never been with an alpha while I was in heat, and I wondered it that was the way every omega felt in that situation. I wasn't sure because I was certain no one had ever felt anything like that.

I couldn't help but think about what it would be like if I accepted Jaxon's offer. If we moved in together. I was certainly excited about seeing this morning.

There was no denying I was attracted to him—and not just because of my heat. But it wasn't just his ridiculously sexy body and that lopsided smile and those gorgeous green eyes that had me hooked. It was everything about him. He was an amazing guy.

Which is why I couldn't take advantage of him. If we could have a real relationship, that would be one thing, but despite what he said I was sure everything Jaxon was doing was for Liam. I was conflicted. On one hand, I knew Jaxon's proposal might be exactly what we needed to get Mrs. Pinder off my back and ensure Liam's adoption, but on the other, it seemed like too much to ask. Plus, I had my heart to protect.

As much as I liked the idea, I just wasn't sure if moving in with Jaxon was the right choice.

Chapter 9 - Jaxon

Kay's had better breakfast than anything else in my opinion.

When I'd stepped out of the bathroom early this morning, it must have woken Liam because the next thing I knew we were face to face in the hall. He'd grinned, realizing I'd stayed there all night. But before he could ask any questions, I'd found a quick way to distract him. Breakfast.

"Thanks so much for bringing me out for breakfast," he said now, his mouth full of the best pancakes in a hundred-mile radius, minimum.

"Yeah, absolutely. I bet you've never gotten ready for school so fast, have you?" I asked with a laugh.

He shook his head, his eyes wide. As soon as the words were out of my mouth, Liam had rushed into the bathroom to get ready. I'd barely had time to check on Bryce—still sleeping soundly—and scribble out a quick note before Liam was waiting at the door.

"I'm so glad you were there this morning. This is awesome," he said.

"Actually, I wanted to talk to you about that." So far, I'd only proposed the details of moving in together and becoming a couple to Bryce, but I wanted Liam's thoughts on the idea. I needed him to be on board too. "I've been thinking, and I really like Bryce. A lot."

Liam grinned. "I know."

I shook my head. Yeah, me staying the night probably wasn't even the first clue. "What would you think about the idea of me and your uncle together?"

"Like dating?" he asked, spearing another huge bite of pancakes with his fork.

"Yeah, something like that," I said with a slight smile.

"I think that's even more awesome!" He chewed his pancakes, and his eyes became thoughtful. "Why are you being so nice, though? I mean, I'm not complaining. It's cool."

I wanted to laugh but managed to keep a straight face. Now he was going for nonchalant.

"Well, part if it is because of what I told you. I like Bryce, but I also want to make sure you're taken care of and you don't go into foster care. I have a good idea of how I can help make that happen." I paused, then went for it. "What would you think about you and Bryce coming to live with me?"

I'd been unwilling at first when my father suggested the idea, not wanting Bryce to find out about shifters until the right moment, but this felt like the right thing to do. Having them at my place was really the best place for all of us.

"My house is pretty big. You'd have all the room you want—it's practically a mansion," I added, tossing that fact in for good measure.

As expected, Liam's eyes lit up and he practically choked on his pancakes.

"Mansion?"

I chuckled. "Yeah. And a huge back yard. Cole lives in the neighborhood too." Neighborhood wasn't exactly the right word to describe the compound the pack lived in. We all had our own homes on the massive property behind the Timberwood Lodge, but we were all close and spent a lot of time together.

"That would be incredible!" he said, glowing now as he finished of his pancakes.

"Then I'll see what I can do to make it happen."

We finished breakfast, and I dropped Liam off at school, then I headed back to Bryce's house.

I let myself in and found him in the kitchen, moving around easily as he cleaned up from last night.

"Hey," I said.

He spun around, surprise on his face. "I didn't hear you come in."

Walking right up to him, I pulled him into my arms. "How are you feeling?"

He looked up at me, more surprise emanating from him as we stood there together. Like he hadn't been expecting this from me this morning. He smiled slowly, a glow about him. He looked sexy as hell, still rumpled from sleep, and that morning-after look was something I could get used to.

"I feel…great," he said with a grin. "I'm not in much pain this morning."

I'd noticed he hadn't seemed to be in much pain last night either, during our interlude and after. I also realized he wasn't in heat any longer.

"Glad to hear that," I replied.

Images of our night together had me immediately thinking about taking advantage of having the house to ourselves. That's when I remembered we hadn't used condoms. At the time I'd been so deep in rut with my omega in heat the thought hadn't even crossed my mind. Did the fact that I'd come inside him have anything to do with how much better he was feeling? I didn't want to discount the possibility—wolf shifter DNA was some pretty potent stuff.

It had me speculating, and I suddenly wanted to find out what more sex with Bryce might do for him. Unfortunately, I had other things I wanted to get squared away first. Primarily my new resolve to get Bryce to move in with me. Now the idea had taken root, I really wanted him where it was safe, surrounded by my pack.

"Do you have any plans for the day?" I asked.

He shook his head.

"Good. Get ready and let's head out to my house. I'd love to show you around and introduce you to some of my family and friends."

Bryce pulled back slightly, hesitation in his hazel eyes. "I'm not sure, Jaxon. I think this might be moving too fast."

Frowning, I tightened my arms around his waist. Why was he so hesitant? Hadn't I shown him last night just how much I wanted him? We were meant to be together, and I was ready to get started. But I could feel his resistance. That's when I remembered he had no clue of the power of our connection, and it wasn't like I could just lay it all out there for him.

Damn it. If I could get him to my place then maybe I could persuade him to move in. He would see how perfect things could be. I decided to change my approach, falling back on what I knew would get him out there.

"Look, at the very least, just come check it out. That way if the social worker questions our relationship, you can at least describe what my place looks like. Show her that I'm here for you and Liam, and that your financial situation is secure."

I felt bad using that to get him out there. I didn't want him to have even more reason to think that what was going on between us wasn't real, but it worked.

"Yeah, I can do that," he said.

"Perfect," I replied, pressing my lips to his forehead. Then I squeezed his ass before giving it a quick slap. I smirked. "Now go get ready before I haul your ass back to bed and we don't ever get out of here."

***

It felt good to walk into the lodge with my mate at my side. Even better than I'd expected. Maybe it was because all my life, finding my mate had been something I wanted. Maybe it was because I felt better equipped to handle my father's proposal of me taking over as pack leader. After all, having a family of my own would make me a better alpha, more capable of leading the rest of the pack.

Or maybe it was just having Bryce with me that felt so good. I certainly loved being here with him. It made me want him by my side all the time.

"Jaxon!" my dad exclaimed, greeting me as I stepped into the doorway of his office. His eyes immediately flew to Bryce, who was standing right behind me. As did three other pairs of eyes. Linc was here, as were some of the other alphas; Gavin Stanton and Jason Meredith.

"Was there a meeting and I didn't get the memo?" I asked, only half joking. I felt Bryce tense behind me, and I reached back to grab his hand. "Guys, this is Bryce Baldwin. My...friend."

Awareness flashed in my father's eyes, but he took the cue about not talking about what Bryce really was to me—my mate.

"Bryce, nice to meet you," he said, standing and coming around the desk. "Greer Parsons, Jaxon's dad."

He offered his hand to Bryce, and I felt more of that tension. Bryce shook my dad's hand, and then cut a quick glance at me, and I knew I needed to tread lightly. Meeting the parents was a huge step, and I'd just tossed him into it.

"Bryce, you've met Linc." I nodded toward my best friend, then gestured to the other alphas that had come to their feet. "This is Gavin Stanton and Jason Meredith. Some of my...associates."

Gavin barely hid a chortle of amusement at my choice of words to describe him. I leveled my gaze on him warningly. He and Jason both caught on quickly—Bryce didn't yet know about shifters.

"It's nice to meet you," Bryce said, stepping forward and extending his hand for the other three men. He held his own, that was for sure. It was intimidating for anyone to be in a room full of alpha wolf shifters, but Bryce seemed to stand a little straighter when he came back to my side.

"So what brings you out here today?" my dad asked, taking a seat again and gesturing for us to sit as well. "Do you want some coffee or anything?"

I shook my head. "No, we were just stopping by on the way to my house so I could show Bryce some of the property. In fact, we'll just head out now and let you get back to business."

The guys exchanged pleasantries with Bryce and we said our goodbyes. As we headed back to my car to drive the rest of the way to my house on the outskirts of the compound, I wondered what he was thinking. If he contemplated what type of "business" me and my "associates" conducted, he didn't ask. In fact, he was pretty quiet for most of the ride. Until we pulled up in front of the giant cabin I called my home.

"Holy shit, Jaxon," he said. "This place is practically a mansion."

I chuckled lightly and climbed from the car to help him out, but by the time I reached his side, he was already stepping from the car himself, barely leaning on his cane.

His eyes were wide as he took it all in. The house was three floors, built into the side of a hill, with wraparound decks and a yard that stretched out until it met the tree line of the forest.

"Come on," I said, taking his free hand. "Let me show you around the cabin."

Bryce laughed. "You call this a cabin?" He shook his head. "Okay, then."

What could I say? I liked nice things. Plus, the house was plenty big to accommodate a large family—something I'd had in mind when I'd had the place built even though I hadn't known if I'd ever meet my fated mate.

I led him inside, noticing how he seemed to make it up the front steps without much of a struggle. Inside, he sucked in a breath, looking around in awe.

The entryway opened up into a huge main room that took up most of the first floor, the open space perfect for having lots of people over—something I'd have to do a lot as pack leader. The entire back wall was made mostly of windows and offered a breathtaking view of the trees in the bright spring morning light. Beyond, the mountains rose up, the tallest of the peaks still white-capped with snow.

Bryce walked straight toward the windows and looked out. I stood back and watched him take it all in, loving the sight of him standing here in my home. It was all too easy to imagine a future together, having him in my home every day and my bed every night. I knew in that moment I would do anything to make that a reality.

"Let me show you upstairs," I said, going to him now and taking his hand again. I felt electricity crackle between us at that touch; my body intensely aware of everything about him.

"Upstairs?" He arched a brow, his voice husky.

I smirked. "Yeah. My bedroom."

Heat blazed in his eyes, and he leaned into me. I breathed him in, and my cock twitched to life, responding to the scent of my mate.

I led him upstairs, and the first thing his attention fell on was the king-sized bed positioned at an angle in the corner. The room was massive, taking up half of the first floor, three sides covered in glass windows. It felt open and airy, almost a part of nature itself. Trees around the perimeter offered plenty of privacy while still letting in a lot of light.

I stepped up behind him and wrapped my arms around his waist, and instantly felt some of his tension leaving him. It made me smile, and I loved knowing he was comfortable here with me.

Turning in my arms, Bryce looked up at me. "This place is amazing."

I grinned. "Glad you like it."

He smiled back, and this time there was less resistance in his gaze. Like he was opening up to me more. There was usually this wall he had erected, and most of the time he came across as guarded. I'd seen him lower that wall maybe a handful of times in the last few days, but when he looked at me now, it was like he let it drop completely.

The wonder and longing on his face made my heart beat faster. I wanted to throw him down on the bed right now and show him just what it could be like for us to be together, here in my home.

But he turned and looked toward a door. "Is that the bathroom?"

"Yeah. Actually that's the best part of this whole place. Let me show you."

Anticipation filled me as I ushered Bryce into my en suite. It shared a wall with the private deck that bordered my room, with a glass French door that also led out. There were lounge chairs, a mini-bar, and a hot tub out on that deck, but inside it was like a spa. A clawfoot tub that could easily accommodate both of us, with room to spare, dominated one wall. The other side featured a giant stone and glass shower with more shower heads than anyone needed, one of them a miniature waterfall. I went over to the control panel beside it and tapped on the screen, activating the shower. Water cascaded down, and the steamers kicked on, and soon the entire enclosure resembled a tropical waterfall paradise.

"Holy shit," Bryce murmured.

"Want to try it out?" I asked, flashing him a mischievous grin and wiggling my eyebrows for good measure.

He laughed. "Only if you insist."

I grabbed him and yanked him against my chest. "Oh, I insist."

Bryce's cane clattered to the floor as he brought his arms between us to clutch my shirt. His cock sprang to life, swelling against mine. I rocked my hips, rubbing against him, and his mouth fell open with a moan.

I wasted no time ridding us both of our clothes. Then I was pulling him into the shower. Steam rose around us, encasing us until it felt like we were the only two people in the world. Everything else melted away as my senses were consumed with my mate standing before me.

I pulled him to me again and crushed my mouth down on his, capturing his lips in a possessive kiss. In this moment, all I could think was, *mine, mine, mine*, and I wanted nothing more than to make him feel good.

I reached between us, taking his cock in my hand. His head fell back as he groaned, and I began to stroke him slowly. Blood pounded through my veins, my pulse rushing in my ears, and my cock swelled even thicker, ready to go. But I wanted this to be about him.

"Let me make you feel good," I murmured against his lips as I backed him slowly against the wall.

Water cascaded from the waterfall, soaking his hair and coursing over the lean planes of his chest. He looked like a fucking sex god in that moment. I clenched my fist around his cock, and his entire body convulsed. Just as I started to go to my knees, he caught my arm. I glanced at him and saw need and determination shining in his eyes. They were dark, his pupils blown out with lust.

"Let me," he said, bringing his hand to my cock and running his fingertips over it, gently, teasingly, until I thought I might come just from his touch. "It's my turn to make you feel good."

Who was I to argue with that?

I let Bryce lead this time—though it took superhuman restraint not to just flip him around and fuck him right where he stood. He moved us slowly until I was the one under the waterfall. He gave my cock a few soft tugs, then harder, causing me to let out a strangled groan.

"Fuck, Bryce," I said. Need coursed through me, especially when he started to drop to his knees. I reached out to help him, seeing the slight unsteadiness in his movements, but he didn't show any signs of pain.

He positioned himself in front of me and wrapped his hand around the base of my cock, then he leaned forward and licked the swollen tip. I growled and wedged my hands in his hair. I wanted to thrust past those lips and feel him swallow around me as I bottomed out. But I restrained myself, barely, surrendering to the pleasure he wanted to give me. He kept his eyes locked on mine as he licked around my cockhead. Then he took me inside that sweet mouth, hollowing his cheeks around me tightly.

"Fuck," I said again, my wolf practically howling, demanding me to take my mate. I gripped his hair even tighter when he began to bob up and down on me, his eyes still on mine. He looked so open in that moment. His face expressing everything he was feeling. Desire. Need. Longing.

I understood the longing most of all. There was nothing more I wanted than to claim this man fully. To make him mine in every way.

My orgasm started to build almost out of nowhere, my balls tightening, tingles shooting up and down my spine, and I couldn't keep myself in check any longer. I pulled my cock from Bryce's mouth with a pop, and he stared up at me, panting. I reached down and grabbed his arms, yanking him up almost roughly. I was trying to be careful with him, not wanting to hurt him, but he didn't seem to object, a desperate moan falling from his lips as I spun him around and pushed him up against the wall, just like I'd imagined.

Though he wasn't in heat his scent surrounded me, growing even stronger as I dipped my fingers between his ass cheeks and found him soaking wet—his slick coating my fingertips.

"Fuck, Bryce," I said again, dropping my forehead to his shoulder. "You're so fucking wet for me."

He instinctively spread his legs wider, and the tip of my cock bobbed just in front of his entrance. I moved his hands above his head and pinned them against the smooth stones with one hand while fisting my cock in the other.

Then I slid inside him, opening him up with my cock. His needy groans echoed in the shower, the raw, guttural sounds spurring me on. I fucked him, hard, digging my fingers of one hand into his hip while I laced the fingers of my other hand with his.

Bryce clenched his ass around me like a vise. I was barely staving off my orgasm, but when I felt my cock begin swelling at the base, I knew I was knotting him again, and I wouldn't have much chance of prolonging it after that. Knotting Bryce was...intense, to say the least. It was unlike anything I'd ever known. The sheer pleasure of being locked so tightly inside my mate, his velvet walls massaging my cock, was enough to drive me mad.

"Ah," he cried out, his head falling back against my shoulder. "Jaxon... God... Yes."

I thrust even deeper inside him, and I felt him convulse as my knot fully swelled.

"Holy shit, what are you doing to me? I've never felt anything like that. What is that—"

"Shh," I murmured in his ear, my breath sending shivers through his body. "Just enjoy it. If it feels this good, don't ask questions." I laughed softly, hoping he would take it at that and not question the knot any further.

I dropped his hands from above his head then gripped his hips. And I fucked him so hungrily he was reduced to incoherent moans of pleasure. When I reached around to grip his cock once more it was like setting fire to a stack of pyrotechnics. His cock throbbed in my hand, and his ass clamped down on me, his orgasm rocketing through him so violently I had to wrap a hand around his waist just to keep him standing.

Then my own release was coursing through my veins, even more intense than last night, my seed pouring from my cock like a jet, filling him. I dropped my forehead to his back again, breathing him in, gasping for breath. We stood there panting, aftershocks wracking both our bodies until my knot finally subsided.

I gently pulled out of him, and he turned, his eyes darting to my cock as if he were looking for some evidence of what he'd felt. Confusion flashed through his eyes, but I distracted him by grabbing a bar of soap and rubbing it over his wet body.

"Let's get you cleaned up," I murmured.

I took my time washing him, carefully, thoroughly, tenderly. He watched me, uncertainty in his eyes again. I didn't like that look there, but I didn't want to press it. When we were both clean, I turned off the water and stepped from the shower, slinging a towel around my waist.

Bryce stepped out after me, holding on to the door for support, but he didn't look like he was struggling. I grabbed a towel and slowly began drying him off.

I looked down at him and smiled. "So, what do you think?"

He half-laughed. "About your shower? I'd give it a positive review."

I chuckled. "That too, but what do you think about my suggestion? What do you think about moving in here with me?"

He smiled softly, but I could sense him putting some of those walls back up. "I think that could be nice…one day. If I think it will help with Liam's adoption."

I frowned, not liking that answer. Why the hell wasn't he just saying yes? There was obviously something between us. Something hot and fierce and full of passion. There was also an underlying bond. I was drawn to him, tied to him, fated to him. He had to feel some of that too, right?

I didn't say anything else as I finished drying him off and helped him into his clothes. My mind was playing back what had happened, trying to figure out why there was a sudden shift in him when he'd seemed so open before and during our shower.

I stiffened, wondering if he was starting to pick up on my secret. If he knew something was different about me. After all, I'd knotted him twice now and I'd told him we were fated mates. I'd introduced him to my pack. What if he was suspecting something about shifters—though, how he'd know I was a shifter specifically was beyond me. But still…

A little warning sounded in the back of my mind. If Bryce didn't fall in love with me like I thought he would, and he found out about shifters, that could put us all in a lot of trouble. I pushed it away. I just had to make him fall for me, that was all there was to it.

However, I wasn't quite sure how to make that happen. I'd been pulling out all the stops, trying my hardest to get him to think of me romantically. Bryce kept saying things were moving too fast, though. Maybe I just needed to be patient and put the brakes on slightly. Not push for too much, too soon. I had a feeling that would be easier said than done.

Chapter 10 - Bryce

Watching Liam on the ball field was incredible. Jaxon was right. He was a natural.

I beamed with pride as Liam walked back to the dugout from the pitcher's mound at the end of the seventh inning. We were in the lead, thanks a lot in part to Liam's skills with pitching—something no doubt due to Jaxon's coaching.

He ran up to Jaxon, who was holding his hand up for a high five, grinning from ear to ear. Jaxon slung his arm around Liam's shoulder, and Liam looked like he would burst from whatever Jaxon whispered to him. Then Jaxon turned around and gave me a disarming smile and wink before huddling up with the kids.

I had a front row seat to the first game of the year, decked out in perfect comfort as the bright April afternoon sun shone down on us. Jaxon had gone out of his way to make sure I was comfortable. He'd brought along a cushioned lawn chair that had a built-in foot rest and pillow, and he'd set up with a cooler next to me if I got thirsty. It felt like he was pampering me, and part of me liked it. A lot.

I watched Jaxon as he coached the kids before they got ready for the next inning, my heart full of something unfamiliar. Jaxon was getting to me, that much was clear. He was steadily tearing down my walls. Making me fall for him. Having a man like him in my life was something I'd never thought possible. Even now, after almost two weeks of Jaxon's attention, it still seemed too good to be true.

The only thing that could make it better would be if I knew this thing between us was real on his part. How did he feel about me? He was so caring and attentive, and wanted me to move in with him, for fuck's sake. It seemed like he wanted me as much as I wanted him, but part of me struggled to accept it. I believed Jaxon when he said he wanted to help me adopt Liam, but would moving in with Jaxon really fix the problem with social services? I just didn't know at this point, and my growing feelings for Jaxon complicated matters.

Before the kids went out to start the next inning, Jaxon snuck out of the dugout and came over to stand beside me, reaching into the cooler for a bottle of water.

"So, you enjoying the game so far?" he asked, wiping the sweat off his brow with his forearm.

Looking up at him, I felt a little dizzy. God, how was he so damn sexy? He smirked when I didn't respond, obviously noticing I was checking him out.

"Yeah," I managed to say. Then I grinned back at him. "Definitely enjoying the show."

Jaxon laughed, then leaned in when he set his water bottle back in the cooler. "You haven't seen anything yet."

I had a feeling he was talking about more than just the game.

The next few innings flew by, our team pretty much sweeping the game. Liam had done an excellent job. I started to push to my feet as the kids ran off the field, cheering and pumping their fists in victory. I was finding it easier to get around the last few days, but when I stood up, another wave of dizziness hit me, this time not just related to Jaxon's proximity. I gripped the back of the chair, but it wasn't that sturdy, and I felt myself losing my balance.

Jaxon was there in a heartbeat. I didn't even know how he made it to me so fast, but he had his arm around my waist holding me before I knew what was happening.

"Whoa, there," he said softly. "You okay?"

I clutched my stomach, which was suddenly roiling. I felt lightheaded and my skin started to tingle uncomfortably. "I don't know," I said, gritting my teeth. "I feel a little woozy all of a sudden."

He watched me carefully, worried. "Maybe we just need to get you home."

"Yeah," I said. "I think this heat is starting to get to me." That had to be it. "Oh, but we promised Liam we'd take him out to celebrate if he won."

Jaxon nodded quickly. "Don't worry about that. I've got a better idea. Let's just get you in the car first."

He helped me to the car and turned it on, blasting cool air. It helped my nausea a little, but not much. I watched as he helped the team gather their things and gave them an after-game congratulatory speech, then he and Liam headed toward the car, Jaxon's arm slung over Liam's shoulders again. They were talking, and Liam was grinning.

When he opened the door and vaulted into the backseat, I didn't even have to ask what he looked so happy about. "Jaxon said he wants to cook at our house instead of going somewhere to eat. Is that okay?"

I smiled up at Jaxon, grateful he hadn't let on to Liam that I wasn't feeling well, and he just winked at me.

"Of course, big man," I said.

Jaxon climbed into the driver's seat and then pulled out onto the road. "Let's hit up the grocery store, what do you say? Steak?"

"Yeah!" Liam exclaimed, pumping his fist in the air.

We'd gone less than a mile when I felt the nausea back in full force.

"Jaxon," I bit out, gripping his arm with one hand and my stomach with the other. "Pull over."

He gave me a worried look and jerked the car to the shoulder of the road. Just in time too. I heaved the door open then got sick all over the grass. Jaxon was out of the car and around on my side in seconds flat, his hands soothing as he rubbed my back and brushed my hair off my forehead. My cheeks burned. I really didn't want him seeing me this way, but it didn't seem like I had much of a choice. Still, he took care of me like he *wanted* to. And I had to say I appreciated it. I felt like shit.

"Do you want me to take you straight home and go back to the store?" he asked, his brow furrowed with concern.

I shook my head. "No. I think I'll be okay now. I don't know what that was about. Maybe the heat," I said weakly, though it hadn't been *that* hot.

He studied me for a few more seconds, then nodded and got me settled in my seat before climbing back behind the wheel. I managed to keep myself together while I waited in the car at the grocery store, but Jaxon had to pull over one more time before we got back to my house. God, this was embarrassing.

"Whose car is that?" Jaxon asked, slowing as we reached my driveway. He pulled up next to the car in question, and I groaned when I saw Mrs. Pinder sitting inside. Could she have any worse timing? She already thought I was barely capable of caring for Liam as it was. Seeing me even weaker than normal wasn't a good look for proving her wrong.

"Is that the social worker?" he asked quietly, and when I nodded he reached over and squeezed my hand. "Don't worry. I've got this."

He climbed out of the car, waving at Mrs. Pinder like they were old friends as he circled around to open my door. He said something to her as she opened her door, but her eyes were on me as Jaxon assisted me out of the car.

She frowned. "Is everything okay?"

I grimaced. "Just feeling a little under the weather, that's all."

She nodded quickly. "I won't stay long then. I just needed to talk to you about the case. The adoption proceedings are coming up soon, and there are a few more things we need to discuss now I've got your financials."

I'd sent them over earlier in the week. Of course she'd want to talk about that while Jaxon was here.

I took a step forward, leaning against Jaxon for support. My legs still felt weak, and my stomach was still roiling. Mrs. Pinder's sharp eyes didn't miss the way he had his arm around me, his touch very familiar.

"And I don't believe I caught your name when I saw you last," she said primly. "You're...close with Mr. Baldwin?"

I opened my mouth to answer her, but Jaxon jumped right in, not missing a beat. "I'm Jaxon Parsons, Bryce's fiancé."

I wondered if my face mirrored Mrs. Pinder's shocked expression, but I couldn't exactly contradict him in front of her. After all, this was part of the plan—or at least a portion of it. We were supposed to convince her we were in a relationship. But engaged?

Jaxon smiled smoothly, bending to kiss the top of my head. "Isn't that right, Bryce?" He turned a disarming grin on her. "We've just gone public with our relationship, but I plan on marrying this man as soon possible. In fact, I'm moving him and Liam into my house even sooner. That way I can look after them both better. Believe me, I plan on taking good care of these two."

He looked back at me, adoration plain on his face, and my heart stuttered. I smiled back, leaning closer to him and resting my head on his shoulder as I wrapped my arms around him. "That's right, baby."

"Let's go inside," Jaxon suggested."

"I won't stay long at all," Mrs. Pinder promised, a complete change in her demeanor now. "I can see you don't feel well."

We went in, and Jaxon and I sat on the couch. "Liam, why don't you go get a shower, buddy?" I asked him.

As soon as he was out of the room, Mrs. Pinder got right to the point. "Really, the only things that would keep this adoption from going smoothly are your financial and physical limitation when it comes to caring for Liam, but if what you're saying is true, this does change things. In your favor, I might add."

For the first time, I saw Mrs. Pinder as possibly not being the bad guy here. She really did just want to make sure Liam was well cared for, and I had the opportunity here, thanks to Jaxon, to prove to her that Liam would be. So I played right along, needing to do my part to make sure this adoption was approved.

"Jaxon is really wonderful with Liam," I told her, though that was every bit the truth. "And Liam loves him."

"And I love Liam," Jaxon added. He was right there saying all the right things, everything she needed to hear, and I wanted too much to believe it was all true.

I sat there and listened as he told Mrs. Pinder how much Liam and I meant to him. That I was an amazing uncle to Liam, everything he needed, and how being in our lives was the best thing that had ever happened to him. I was almost shocked by the level of sincerity in his voice. Either he was an amazing actor, or he meant the things he was saying. God, how I wanted it to be the latter.

Within just a few minutes, Jaxon seemed to have satisfied Mrs. Pinder to the point that she stood up and gave me a genuine smile. "Mr. Baldwin, I have to say, this is all wonderful news. I can honestly say that I can pretty much guarantee the adoption being granted in light of this new information."

Jaxon squeezed my hand. "Well, I'm happy to hear that. Because there's truly nothing to worry about as far as finances or Bryce's ability to care for Liam are concerned. I'll be right there every step of the way, supporting them both in any way I can."

"I'll be in touch before long," she said, gathering her things. We started to get up, but she waved her hand. "I can show myself out. Have a nice evening."

Then she was gone.

I slumped on the sofa, still feeling queasy, but also feeling like a huge weight had been lifted off my shoulders. Jaxon's plan had worked. Mrs. Pinder had all but assured me the adoption would be approved now.

"How are you feeling?" Jaxon asked, still holding my hand.

"Tired," I admitted.

"How about you just take a nap, and I'll take care of everything else. By the time you wake up, I'll have dinner ready."

"That sounds...amazing."

Jaxon smiled, then helped me to my feet and toward my bedroom. The shower was still running, and I could hear Liam singing *'Take Me Out to the Ball Game'*, his little voice echoing off the bathroom walls.

I chuckled. "He had an amazing day today."

"*I* had an amazing day. I can't tell you how happy it makes me to be part of your lives," Jaxon said, echoing what he'd said to Mrs. Pinder.

As I sank down on the bed, Jaxon beside me, his arm still around me, I wondered again how much of what he said was the real truth. Turning to him, my brows furrowed, I just put it out there.

"Jaxon, did you really mean what you said to Mrs. Pinder?"

"Every word," he said without hesitation, his gaze piercing mine. I searched his eyes and found nothing there but raw honesty.

"But... I thought this was just about Liam."

"How many times do I have to tell you I really want to be with you, Bryce? Truly with you. In every way."

I gave him a small smile. "I guess one more time wouldn't hurt."

He laughed lightly, but then became serious again. He shifted to face me fully on the bed and framed my face with his hands.

"Bryce Baldwin, I want you. I want to spend every day with you at my side, and every night with you in my bed. Having Liam is just icing on the cake. But even if that weren't a factor, I'd still want you. How could I not? You're everything I could possibly want. I love you, Bryce."

I sucked in a deep breath at his confession, shock and ecstasy mingling together and leaving me speechless.

He loved me? After only a couple of weeks? But his confession forced me to acknowledge what I was feeling. I hadn't been able to put a name to it before, but I knew what it was now, without a doubt. Love. I wasn't just falling for Jaxon Parsons. I was already in love with him. My eyes pricked and my throat tightened as I swallowed back tears of sheer joy. Then I found my voice again.

"I love you too, Jaxon."

I could feel his relief as if it were palpable. His shoulders sagged as if he'd been carrying a huge weight, but the grin that covered his face was nothing but delighted.

I swallowed again and shook my head slightly. "Are you sure this isn't too soon?" I couldn't help but ask. "I mean, we've barely just gotten to know each other."

He shook his head adamantly. "It's not too soon. When you know, you know. And I've known from the first minute I set eyes on you that you were meant to be mine. We're fated mates, remember?"

My brow furrowed again. I wanted to ask him what he meant by that phrase. That was the second time he'd used it. Maybe it was just his way of saying he loved me. I didn't want to question it, not when he was saying everything I could ever hope to hear; that he cared for me—really and truly cared, and that he wanted to be with me. I gazed at him in wonder, marveling over how I could be so lucky.

His face softened, and he leaned in, pulling me close as he settled his lips over mine in a long, slow, sensual kiss that had my entire body feeling weak.

"Get some rest," he whispered when he finally pulled away. "I'll be here when you wake up."

He got me all tucked into bed, then gave me another sweet kiss before drawing my curtains and walking out, tossing one more affectionate grin over his shoulder as he shut the door gently behind him.

I drifted off, feeling more content and at ease than I had in a long time.

Chapter 11 - Jaxon

"Nothing like a lazy Sunday, am I right?" I grinned at Liam, who was curled up on the couch between Bryce and me, still in his pajamas even though it was almost noon.

"The best," he agreed, grabbing the remote to click 'continue' on the screen. We'd been binge watching his favorite cartoons all morning, just hanging out and laughing and taking it easy, and I had to say, it was shaping up to be one of the best days of my life. Just being with these two made me feel whole, and not only had I admitted the truth of my feelings to Bryce—he felt the same way.

I rested my arm along the back of the couch, brushing my fingers through the ends of Bryce's hair and teasing his neck. He shot me a look, full of heat, and I smiled. Last night had been another incredible round of sex. Every time I was with Bryce, it felt impossibly better than the last.

As Liam stared at the television, transfixed, I winked at Bryce then stood up. "I think I'll just clean up from breakfast."

"I'll help you," he said quickly, pushing to his feet. Liam barely seemed to notice as we gathered the dishes littering the coffee table and carried them into the kitchen.

Bryce still seemed to be doing well physically. He'd had that bout of sickness yesterday, but he'd seemed more or less back to normal today. Though he had turned his nose up at my attempt at breakfast.

"That looks disgusting," he'd said, eyeing the stack of jellybean pancakes I'd made. It had ended up like more of an ice cream sundae with all the trimmings I'd scrounged up. Whipped cream—some of which I'd saved for later—chocolate syrup, sprinkles and chocolate chips, and to top it all off, cherries.

I'd just laughed and offered him plain toast. He'd jumped at that idea without hesitating. Maybe his stomach was still bothering him, but he seemed to be doing great right now as we cleaned up the dishes together.

"We make a good team," I remarked as he dried off the last pan and handed it to me to put away. I reached up to put it in the cabinet, noticing some cobwebs near the ceiling as I did. "Hey, where are your cleaning supplies?"

"Jaxon," he protested "I'm not going to have you cleaning my house now too. You've done enough."

"I want to do it, Bryce," I replied, brushing a quick kiss on his lips. "Now sit your ass down and tell me where your cleaning stuff is."

"Only if I get to watch you do it shirtless," he said, and I laughed. I loved it when this more playful side of Bryce came out.

I grabbed him and pulled him against me, then leaned down and nipped at his bottom lip. "Deal."

He grinned, then pointed out the utility closet before sitting down at the kitchen table. Not to go back on an agreement, I stripped my shirt off and gave him another wink before getting down to business.

I spent the next hour cleaning all the hard to reach spots in Bryce's kitchen, feeling his gaze boring into me the entire time. We laughed and joked as well, and I relaxed into the intimacy of just sharing these small things with him. All this domesticity might seem dull to some people, but to me it just made my chest swell with happiness. This was exactly what I'd always wanted. To just enjoy being with the man I loved and everything that came along with it.

I opened the windows as I cleaned, letting in the fresh air. It was a gorgeous day outside, and it seemed like spring was in full bloom. The scent of honeysuckle drifted in, mingling with the citrus cleaners I'd used.

Just then Liam came dashing into the room. He must have been tired of watching cartoons because he looked out the window then back at me with a hopeful smile on his face. "Can we go outside and play?"

"I think that's a great idea. Want to play catch?"

Liam's eyes shone brightly. "Yeah!" Then he was darting off, presumably to grab some equipment.

"Jaxon, you don't have to—"

"Will you stop saying that? I want to do all this for you guys. Maybe you'll start to see that soon enough. I enjoy this," I added, crossing to him and running my knuckles along his cheek. He smiled at me, still somewhat in awe. I got that. I was feeling the same thing. Awe, gratitude that I'd found my mate, and excitement about what the future held for us. I couldn't wait to move him into my place. There was just one thing keeping me from doing that, though—letting him in on my little secret.

I had to tell him I was a shifter. Before, that thought had terrified me. I'd worried he might ostracize me and even cause some difficulties for the pack. But after this weekend, after what we'd shared, and knowing he loved me, I was no longer concerned.

It was time to tell my mate I was a shifter. Then we could really move forward into the bright future I was certain we had waiting for us.

***

Monday morning I got up earlier than both Bryce and Liam and headed into the kitchen. I wanted to make today special. The day I told my mate I was a shifter. I had it all planned out, but I wanted everything to be a surprise. So I got to work putting together a picnic brunch before the sun even rose.

I managed to finish it all up and get breakfast going by the time I heard the boys stirring. My boys. They were mine. My heart thudded faster knowing I was close to having the family I'd dreamed of. The entire weekend had been perfect, and I didn't want to spend another night apart from them. Hopefully after today, I wouldn't have to.

"Hey, buddy," I said to Liam as he ambled into the kitchen and grabbed the plate I'd just made for him. "How did you sleep?" He looked a little more tired than usual.

He shrugged and grabbed a fork, gathering up some eggs. "Okay. I had a bad dream."

I frowned and pulled out a chair, spinning it around and straddling it as I faced him. "Want to talk about it?"

He glanced toward the doorway, like he was looking for Bryce. When Liam didn't see him, he turned his gaze back to me. "It was about my mom," he said, his voice almost a whisper.

My heart skipped a beat. I still didn't know the full story about what happened to Liam's mother. All I knew was that whatever it was had also caused Bryce's injuries. I'd wanted to ask, but I hadn't wanted to push him. I figured if it was something he wanted to talk about, he'd prefer to be the one to bring it up. I reached out and squeezed Liam's shoulders. "I can't say I know what it's like to lose a parent, but I can kind of relate."

He looked up at me, curious. "What do you mean?"

"I was adopted," I told him. "Never knew my birth parents, and my adoptive father had lost his mate before I was born. So I only grew up with one parent too."

He nodded. "It's why you want to take care of us."

I paused, not sure what to say with that. I hadn't really thought of it that way, but Liam had a good point. I definitely wanted to make sure Liam had everything he needed, but I'd not actually considered the underlying reason was because of my own circumstances.

"Does that bother you?" I asked, knowing this kid had an adult's wisdom, and deserved complete transparency from me. "Are you afraid I might try to replace your mom?"

He shook his head. "No. Not at all." He smiled then, shaking the weight off his shoulders. "I'm really happy you're here, Jaxon."

"Me too, buddy," I said, ruffling his hair. "Me too."

A couple of seconds later, Bryce came in, freshly showered and dressed. "You ready?" he asked Liam.

Liam jumped up and grabbed his backpack. "Yep!"

I walked up to Bryce and kissed him good morning, right in front of Liam, who giggled and raced out of the house.

"Good morning, gorgeous," I murmured.

"Good morning," he replied with a smile, wrapping his arms around my neck. "I see you got Liam all taken care of, yet again."

"I did. Let's get that boy to school." I paused, looking down into his eyes. "After we drop him off, I'd really like to talk to you."

His brow furrowed in curiosity, but he simply nodded. "Sure."

I grinned. "Great." Then I led him to the car, which I'd already packed up with everything we'd need today. It felt so natural to drive up to the school together with Bryce and Liam and see Liam off to school. Like he was ours. I couldn't keep the goofy smile off my face thinking about us as a family.

"What?" Bryce asked, turning to me once Liam got out of the car and darted across the school yard.

"Just thinking about how lucky I am."

Bryce flushed but his smile was pleased. "I think I'm the lucky one here."

I chuckled. We were both lucky, and we had fate on our side.

"You want to go for a drive?" I asked, pulling out of the school parking lot.

"I thought you wanted to talk."

"Yeah, but I know just the spot. We can talk, and...other things." I shot him a grin.

"How can I say no to that?" he asked with a laugh.

I rolled down the windows and headed toward the highway on the west of Timberwood. There was a scenic drive along the coast, and I knew it would be gorgeous this time of day with the weather we were having. The wind whipped in, blowing through our hair as I turned onto the highway and cruised at an easy pace.

Every time I looked at Bryce, smiling as he watched the ocean sparkle to our left, my heart felt full. I turned on the music, and we fell into companionable silence.

But after a few minutes, I saw Bryce stiffen beside me. "Where are we going?" he asked, his eyes darting around frantically.

"Bryce?" I frowned, reaching for his hand. "Are you okay?"

His skin felt clammy, and a shudder ran through him.

"Bryce?" Now I was worried. He started breathing heavily, practically gasping, his eyes wild. He began shaking harder now, muttering to himself. With a quick glance in the rearview mirror, I jerked the car to the side of the road. Was he feeling sick again? He'd seemed fine since Saturday, but as I looked at his pale face and saw how shaken he looked, I knew this wasn't illness. Something was very wrong. It was almost like he was having a panic attack. I squealed to a stop and turned to Bryce, gripping his face. "What's wrong, baby?" I asked, not sure what to do.

He shook his head frantically, his mouth moving but no sound coming out. He was staring ahead at a rise in the road, a hill that opened up to a great view of the ocean, just where I wanted to take him.

"Look at me," I said, and his eyes finally settled on me. They were wild and frantic. Full of fear.

"I—I can't—" He swallowed hard, his eyes going back to the hill. Another shudder started to wrack his body.

There was something about where we were that was causing him to react like this. The only thing I could think to do was turn around and head in the opposite direction. I kept my gaze on the road as I sped back toward town, toward Bryce's house, but I cut glances at him and kept telling him he'd be okay, telling him to breathe, that I had him. He was safe.

I didn't know what was going on, but that was something I would make sure of; that whatever had him upset never did again.

As soon as I pulled into his driveway, I darted around the car and helped him out. He leaned on me more heavily now, his limbs unsteady, and I pulled him in tightly to my side, not even worrying with the cane. His legs faltered. Fuck that. I swung him up in my arms and carried him the rest of the way into his house, straight to his bed.

I quickly got him settled, murmuring softly to him all the while, reassuring him that I had him. That I was here. Then I climbed into bed beside him and wrapped my arms around him, holding him to my chest. I could hear his heart thundering.

"Just breathe, baby," I whispered, stroking his back.

Eventually, the shakes subsided and he began to breathe more evenly, slowly drawing ragged breaths in and out. I remained silent other than my soft murmurs, not wanting to push him if he wasn't ready to talk about this. However, I was prepared to wait it out. I needed to know what just happened.

Finally, he drew in one more deep breath before turning to look at me. "I'm sorry."

"What the hell do you have to be sorry for?" I captured his cheeks in my palms. "I just want to know if you're okay."

He nodded slowly, huffing out a breath. "I am. I'm just sorry that happened. I never expected it to affect me like that, but I haven't been back there since..."

He squeezed his eyes shut and the muscle in his jaw throbbed. I let him have a moment to gather himself. When he opened his eyes again he looked steadier. I reached for his hand and gently held it.

"That hill we were driving toward. That was where my sister died."

I felt an icy chill race through me. Oh my god. No wonder he'd been so upset.

"I... I was driving..."

"Shh," I said, lowering my forehead to his. "You don't have to talk about it if you don't want to."

He shook his head. "No. I want to. I need to, I think. I haven't talked about this with anyone other than my therapist. I think it would be good for me. And..." His gaze softened on me. "I trust you."

My stomach did a little flip at that. He was admitting he trusted me with something he didn't share easily. Just like I wanted to do with him by telling him I was a shifter. I felt even more sure that we were headed on the right path now.

"Thank you for trusting me," I said, softly. "But only if you want to talk about it."

He nodded. "My sister. She was my twin. The closest person to me in the whole world. Part of my soul, though I don't know if you can understand that."

I understood it more than he realized. Because that's how I already felt about him. Like he was the other half of *my* soul.

"I was driving her back into town to get some construction supplies—I'd promised her I would fix her deck but I'd forgotten to grab things in town before I went out to her place. Liam wasn't with us, thank god. It was already dark, and the moon wasn't out." He swallowed hard, and I rubbed slow circles on his back.

Another deep breath. "As we topped that hill, my headlights caught a wolf standing in the middle of the road."

That icy shiver I'd felt earlier was back, now a cold chill deep in my bones. A wolf?

"I swerved to avoid it, just at the top, and I didn't see the headlights on the other side of the hill. We ran head first into a semi-truck."

Oh god. My eyes widened and I sucked in a sharp breath. This was so much worse than I could have imagined. I had no idea his sister had been killed in such a horrific way. And from the sound of it, he blamed himself.

"Bryce," I said, staring intently into his eyes. "You know it wasn't your fault."

His lips pressed into a flat line. "Not completely." He paused, his eyes filling with a mixture of guilt and anger. At himself? At the wolf? My stomach clenched, horror filling me at the prospect. Just the idea that a wolf was involved in the accident... Had it been a regular wolf? Or a shifter? I couldn't even process the sheer horror of that possibility.

He jerked his gaze away from mine. "We flipped multiple times," he explained, his voice flatter now. "Ending up in a ditch and eventually slamming into a tree. Lorelei didn't make it, and now I can barely walk."

I pulled him to me, whispering his name over and over, and all his pent-up emotions came pouring out. His body shook, this time with sobs as he broke down. I let him cry it out, hoping it was good for him, that getting all of this out there made him feel a little better.

There was so much more he'd had to deal with than I'd realized. He was dealing with guilt, blaming himself for the loss of his twin. My heart pounded. He also blamed that wolf. I could tell. And if it had been a shifter...

How the hell could I ever tell Bryce about myself now?

Chapter 12 - Bryce

3:32

That's what the glowing red of my bedside alarm clock read.

I didn't know what had woken me up from my deep sleep. I closed my eyes and rolled from my side to my back. My arm brushed up against warm skin.

Eyes flying open again, I caught my breath when I turned my head slightly and saw Jaxon's sleeping form next to me. He'd stayed the night?

I didn't remember him crawling into bed next to me. I really must have been sleeping like the dead. Though it was better than the alternative—staying awake replaying the car accident over and over. Maybe my mind had sought to shield me from it and just shut off.

I tried to recall what had happened yesterday after Jaxon brought me home after my panic attack. I'd told him all about Lori and the accident. Made it clear it was my fault. Then I'd broken down in his arms. All that was clear, but it didn't explain why he was still here.

I'd seen the look of horror on his face when I'd told him what happened—how Lori had died because of me. Jaxon apparently thought I was to blame too. And I was, obviously. So why was he still here?

Snippets of the day before came back to me. Jaxon going to pick up Liam from school. Making sure he had both an afternoon snack and dinner. Playing catch again in the yard. I remembered Jaxon checking up on me several times through the course of the afternoon and evening. Each time when I wasn't actually out of it, I'd pretended to be asleep, not wanting to have to see the look on his face now he knew the truth.

I gazed at him again. He was sleeping, his breath shallow, his face relaxed. I took the opportunity to really study him. The wide set of his jaw, his full lips. The dark lashes that rested on his defined cheekbones. I almost reached out to brush his dark waves from his forehead, but then caught myself. I didn't want to wake him.

My mind working now, I knew I wouldn't be falling back asleep any time soon. I slid from the bed as quietly as I could, reaching for my cane, then limped out the door. With one final glance at Jaxon, I pulled the door shut then went into the kitchen.

With a heavy sigh, I hobbled to the counter and pulled out a teacup then set the kettle on the stove. Maybe if I drank something calming I might be able to go back to sleep. It might also help settle some of the churning I felt in my stomach, though I wasn't sure if that was a residue from the nausea I'd felt Saturday or if it was just my nerves.

As I waited for the water to boil I leaned against the counter and squeezed my eyes shut. God, how I wished I could take back everything that happened yesterday. I hadn't known where Jaxon was taking me, but the minute I'd seen that hill, I'd lost my shit. I hadn't had a breakdown like that yet, even more than six months after the crash. Just being in the same vicinity shouldn't have had such an impact on me, but maybe I hadn't fully worked through my emotions yet.

Well, there was no maybe about it. My therapist had told me there wasn't much more she could do for me until I was able to open up about what happened and face my problems head-on. While I had to admit that coming clean to Jaxon had felt cathartic, now I regretted it.

Would this make him finally see me the way I saw myself? What if he'd changed his mind about me? What if I'd lost him? I already didn't understand why a man like him would love someone like me. I'd pretty much written that possibility off, yet here he was. Still in my bed. He said he loved me. That he wanted to be with me, and I believed him, but I couldn't shake the feeling that something had changed in Jaxon yesterday... That look on his face.

I shook my head as the kettle began to whistle. I quickly removed it from the heat, pouring the steaming water over my tea bag. I turned off the burner, and then made my way over to the kitchen table, lowering myself carefully in case my legs acted up. They didn't seem to be bothering me much right now, though.

I heard a noise behind me and turned in my chair. Jaxon. He was leaning against the door frame watching me.

"Couldn't go back to sleep," I muttered before bringing the teacup to my lips, not caring it was still scalding hot. I needed something to do with my hands, my mouth.

I felt more than heard Jaxon push from the wall and cross the floor. The air around me seemed to thicken with awareness. His mere presence sent my entire body into overdrive.

Pulling out a chair next to me, Jaxon sank into it then reached out for my hand. He wove his fingers through mine, holding me gently. I braced for the worst. Maybe this would be it. Maybe he finally realized he didn't want to be with me, and he wanted to get it out of the way now. Part of me realized that was ridiculous, especially in light of everything Jaxon had said and done so far. Still, I simply couldn't get that look of horror on his face out of my mind. With it came a wave of crushing guilt. I didn't deserve him.

"Are you okay?" he asked softly. A little reserved. A lot concerned.

He studied me closely, his brows drawn together. I took a minute to soak him in before answering. The vulnerable twist of his mouth, his deep green eyes. The strength of his shoulders and arms that belied just how gentle he could be.

Then he reached up with his other hand and ran his knuckles over my cheek. "How are you feeling, Bryce?" A tender smile pulled at his lips.

That wasn't what I'd expected. After a pause, I shrugged. "I guess I still feel a little nauseous, but I'm not really in a lot of pain, if that's what you mean." Not a lot of physical pain, at least. Emotional pain was another matter altogether.

"It's been several days," he murmured, his eyes darting back and forth between mine. "You're still feeling nauseous?"

I nodded. "It comes and goes. Maybe I just caught a bug or something and it wasn't the heat, after all."

Jaxon narrowed his eyes slightly. "But it hasn't gone away completely?"

"No," I admitted. "I'd hoped the tea would help settle my stomach. Maybe I should eat some crackers or something."

Out of nowhere, Jaxon grinned, his eyes lighting up.

"What?" I asked, confused.

Instead of answering, Jaxon captured my face in his hands and leaned in to kiss me. He pressed his mouth hard against mine, breathing me in, then released me. I gasped for a breath. I hadn't expected that.

Then he was up and scouring my pantry. "Ah, here we go!" He came back to the table with a box of crackers. "I'll be right back."

He rushed out of the room and I heard him doing something in my room. When he reappeared in the kitchen, he was fully dressed, keys in his hand. He came up to me again and kissed me just like before—hard, animated, determined.

I was so confused. "Where are you going?"

He just smiled. "Just stay right here and don't move. I won't be long."

Then he was gone. What the hell was going on? I sat there for a few minutes, dumbfounded, then decided I might as well finish my tea before it got cold. I managed to get a couple crackers down too, which helped some of the acidic feeling in my stomach.

I glanced at the clock when I was done. Jaxon had been gone twenty minutes. Pushing from the chair, I took my cup to the sink. Where had he gone? He said he wouldn't be long, but where did someone dart off to at nearly four in the morning without explanation?

I busied myself with making a grocery list, figuring I should at least not waste the quiet time before Liam woke up. It wasn't like I'd be going back to sleep any time soon. But forty-five minutes later, Jaxon still hadn't returned. He'd been gone just over an hour already. Maybe I should go ahead and take a shower and get ready for the day. I had plenty of time to cook breakfast for Liam at this rate. We wouldn't be running late for once—though being late hadn't been an issue since Jaxon had been around taking care of us.

I sighed and started to trudge toward the bathroom, but then stopped when I heard the front door. Jaxon scurried inside, shutting it quietly behind him. He smiled when he saw me and rushed up, gathering me in his arms and kissing me, a little less urgently this time but no less passionately. Seriously, what was going on?

I broke away. "Where did you go?"

Jaxon grinned and held up a small paper bag. "Sorry I was gone so long. I thought I could run down to the corner store, but you wouldn't believe how hard it is to find a shop at this hour that sells these things."

He reached into the bag and pulled out a box. My eyes widened. I laughed nervously. "Is that what I think it is?"

Jaxon beamed. "Yep. A pregnancy test. Here. Take it. Let's find out."

I was stunned. Speechless, even. Jaxon thought I was pregnant? No way. I shook my head slowly. I couldn't be pregnant.

"Just take the test," Jaxon said, excitement radiating from him. I took a second to process that. He was *excited* about the idea of me being pregnant.

"Jaxon, I—" I swallowed hard. "I couldn't be..."

"Come on." Jaxon laced his fingers with mine and pulled me into the bathroom. He pushed the little box into my hand and wrapped my fingers around it, then gave me an encouraging smile before slipping out the door and shutting it behind him.

I stood there, staring down at the box, my mind reeling. I could hear Jaxon pacing outside the door of the bathroom.

"How's it going?" he asked in a stage-whisper.

"Um," I whispered back. "Fine."

Fine. That was the opposite of how I felt. Honestly, I didn't know how I felt about the likelihood of being pregnant. I'd never actually considered being a father—other than to Liam. I'd pretty much resigned myself to it just being the two of us. Then Jaxon had come along and flipped everything I knew on its head. In every way, apparently.

I continued staring at the box, wondering how this was possible. I mean, I obviously knew how, technically, but how had I been irresponsible enough to not take precautions? I remembered I'd only briefly thought of condoms that night I'd been in heat. Right before I'd become completely lost to the sensations Jaxon sparked in me. Every time after that I'd become equally lost in him. Fully wrapped up in everything about him, losing all sense of reason. I blew out a breath. And now I was about to find out what exactly that meant for me.

Jaxon rapped lightly on the door and twisted the doorknob. "Are you okay?" His voice was anxious, and I had to laugh a little.

"Yes. Now can you please go stand somewhere other than right outside the bathroom so I can actually do this thing?"

His warm chuckle trickled through the thin door. "Right. Okay. I'll be right here on the couch then."

I listened as his footsteps faded, then stared dubiously at the box. I had no idea what to do with this thing.

"Well, here goes nothing," I muttered, ripping open the packaging and pulling out a sheet of instructions. "What the hell?"

The instructions were printed in the tiniest of fonts, covering both sides of the paper. Surely it wasn't this complicated to take a pregnancy test. Right? I sat down on the closed lid of the toilet and found the English section, and then read over the directions three times.

Exhaling slowly, I set the paper aside. Okay, I could do this. Meticulously, I followed the instructions. Didn't want to allow any margin for error. Then I washed my hands, set a timer on my watch, and set the test on the back of the toilet before walking out of the bathroom.

Jaxon bolted to his feet and immediately came up to me. He took both my hands in his, his gaze scouring my face for some clue. "Well?"

I managed a smile. "It takes three minutes."

"You've been in there for ten," he exclaimed.

I shrugged. "Yeah, well… I wanted to make sure I did it right."

We stood there, staring at each other silently, and I tried to understand his reaction. Ever since he'd jumped up from the kitchen table an hour and half ago, he'd seemed nothing but enthusiastic.

"Jaxon, how are you okay with this?" I finally forced myself to ask.

"Are you kidding me right now?" He pulled me close to him and stared down at me, piercing me with his emerald gaze. "I told you, Bryce. I love you. I want a life and a future with you, and all that comes with it."

"Yeah, but it's all so—"

"Soon?" He chuckled. "Yeah. You've mentioned that before, but when you know, you know."

He'd said *that* before, when he'd said we were fated mates—his version of soul mates I guessed. But hearing him say it again filled my heart with warmth. All my doubts from earlier seemed to evaporate as I stood in front of him. The man I loved. Who apparently loved me too.

We might be having a baby together. It was crazy, but I couldn't help feeling some of Jaxon's enthusiasm pouring into me. What would that be like? To be a real family with Jaxon? It was more than I ever could have dreamed for myself.

"Okay, I can't wait any longer," he said abruptly, pulling me back toward the bathroom.

I glanced at my watch. "We still have another minute to go."

He shook his head. "Doesn't matter."

He strode right into the bathroom and picked up the test. He frowned at it, then looked up at me. "What do two blue lines mean?"

Oh. My. God.

I grabbed the instructions just to be sure, and it was there plain as day.

"Positive," I whispered. "It means I'm pregnant."

Shock flooded my body, along with a warmth that swirled through my chest.

Jaxon let out a loud whoop, grinning like a loon and gathering me up in his arms. I could feel his heart pounding against mine. I laughed. I didn't know how else to react, the mixture of amazement and joy filling me.

"Oh my god, Jaxon," I said, pulling back to look at him.

His smile broadened, then he crushed his mouth to mine. I lost myself in his kiss. It was sweet, but also hot, teeming with passion. I kissed him back, pouring all my emotions into it, completely overwhelmed. Jaxon seemed elated, and I had to admit, even though I'd never thought about having a baby, I was just as excited now it was starting to sink in. My heart was so full of love for this man I thought it might burst.

Jaxon broke the kiss just as Liam's door creaked open. He stood there in his pajamas, rubbing his eyes, his blond hair sticking up all over the place.

"What's all the noise?" he asked, his voice groggy.

Jaxon went right to him and knelt down in front of him, placing his hands on Liam's shoulders. "Liam, Bryce and I just found out some amazing news."

That got his attention. Liam's swiveled his head between the two of us, his eyes alert now. "What? I wanna know!"

Jaxon grinned. "Bryce is pregnant. We're having a baby!"

"What!" Liam's screech filled the room, and I had to laugh.

"Yep. You're going to be a big brother," I said, grinning so much I thought my face might crack.

Liam's eyes went wide. "A big brother..."

He would be. Because we would be a true family. I'd move him and Bryce out to the homestead on the pack lands, into my house. We'd also have a new addition to our little family. It seemed too good to be true.

Then Liam was throwing himself into my arms. "I've always wanted to be a big brother." He sounded choked up, and I had to swallow a couple times.

Bryce came over to us, resting his hand on Liam's back. Then he knelt down beside me. I reached out for him instinctively to help him down, but he didn't seem to need too much help at the moment. I put my arm around him and pulled him to my side, and he wrapped his arms around both me and Liam.

"I'm glad to see you're thrilled about it," he said softly to Liam.

"Thrilled? This is the best news ever!" He pulled away from our hug and started jumping around the room. "I hope it's a boy. Then I can teach him everything about baseball. Or wait, no. I hope it's a girl! Then I can be a protective big brother. No, wait..."

I laughed. "You're going to be a great big brother no matter what."

Bryce turned to me, his eyes shining in wonder. He shook his head slightly, like he was still trying to process this. I was still a little in shock myself, but I'd had a little more time than him to get used to the idea. As soon as I realized he'd been nauseous for the last three days, I'd started to suspect. He'd also had something a little different about his scent. I'd picked up on that Saturday, and occasionally throughout the day yesterday, but I hadn't recognized it for what it was. His pheromones had changed. I knew that now. And when I'd taken a good whiff of him at the kitchen table this morning, it had pretty much confirmed my suspicions.

Reaching down, I placed my hand gently on Bryce's lower abdomen, still flat and lean-muscled. Soon I'd be able to feel my baby in there. My baby!

The idea of finding my mate and becoming a father in such a short time might have scared some men, but this was everything I'd ever hoped for, and I'd found it with Bryce, the strongest, most selfless man I'd ever met.

I leaned in and captured his lips in a soft but innocent enough kiss since Liam was present. "I love you," I murmured against his mouth, and I felt him quiver. He looked up at me again as I pulled back, his eyes shining with emotion.

Liam was chattering away about how much help he could be, and I chuckled as I stood and helped Bryce to his feet. "Be careful about volunteering, or I may just put you on diaper duty."

He grinned, not at all put off. "Does this mean we can move in with you now?" He turned to Bryce. "Please?"

I wrapped my arms around Bryce from behind, letting my hands settle on his belly, rubbing soft circles. He leaned back against me, relaxing a bit.

"We'll see what happens," he said.

They'd end up living with me, there was no question there. It was just a matter of timing now. I just needed to figure out when. A dark cloud started to hover over me as I remembered I'd hoped to have all my secrets out in the open by now. I had to tell him for sure, and I couldn't wait long, but I was uncertain how to go about it. I shoved the cloud away, wanting to enjoy this moment and not think about anything else for the time being. I'd figure it all out later, somehow.

"I can't wait for you to move out to the homestead," I said, assuring Liam. Bryce didn't object, so that was something.

Liam ran off to get ready for school, and I turned Bryce to face me. I couldn't stop touching his stomach. I knew I was being a sap, but who cared? Not me. I was freaking ecstatic. I didn't think Bryce minded the attention either by the way he was grinning at me.

I pulled him into another kiss now we were alone. Slower, deeper. Full of tenderness. I wanted him to know how happy I was about this. Leave no room for doubt in his mind. He'd doubted things between us enough already, and I wanted to reassure him I was here to stay. That we were meant to be, and that I was more than thrilled about this baby.

Bryce pulled back suddenly, then yawned widely, his hand coming up to cover his mouth.

"Tired?" I asked.

He nodded, his eyes sleepy now. "Guess I'm not used to waking up at three in the morning."

"Come on, let's get you back to bed. I'll get Liam off to school. You need to get your rest."

He leaned against me, as if his tiredness was hitting him hard all of a sudden. I swept him up in my arms and carried him right to his bed.

"I can walk, you know," he said wryly before yawning again.

"Yes, but you're exhausted. After all, you are growing our baby in there."

He smiled up at me and murmured, "Our baby."

I didn't miss the spark of joy in his eyes as he said it. I kissed him again, then settled him on the bed before taking his hand. I really wanted him to be sure of how much this meant to me.

"Bryce, I couldn't be happier to have you as the father of my child," I said, staring into his eyes. "I love you."

He smiled. "I love you too."

I didn't think I'd ever get tired of hearing that.

"I need to run some errands after I drop Liam off at school. But you get some sleep, and I'll be back in just a few hours, okay?"

Bryce nodded, his eyes already sliding shut.

I headed to the kitchen and got breakfast ready for Liam. When he came in, dressed for school, he came up to me and threw his arms around me again.

"I'm so happy, Jaxon."

I ruffled his hair. "Me too, buddy. I can't wait."

"And we can really move into your house?" he asked.

I nodded. "You really can." I just had to figure that part out. I knew my father wouldn't want humans who weren't aware of shifters living on the homestead. I'd just have to talk to him, hope he could help me figure out the situation.

I got Liam off to school, then turned my car onto the road leading out into the woods where the lodge was located. I knew I'd find my dad in his office at this time. I couldn't wait to see the look on his face when I told him he was going to be a grandfather. He'd be excited too, no doubt.

As I drove down the two-lane road into the forest, I thought about what I would say. What he might tell me. I definitely needed his guidance. This changed a lot of things. Before, I'd thought I'd have plenty of time to talk to Bryce about the existence of shifters. I mean, I'd planned on telling him yesterday, but at that point the only reason was because I wanted to move him out to my place. I was simply ready for that next step in our relationship.

But now we had a time constraint and things weren't so simple, not with the way Bryce was so upset about the accident and his sister's death. *And that wolf.* I sighed. Yeah, things were complicated, alright.

Plus there was the issue of Bryce's health. He seemed strong enough, and he got around okay, but what if his injuries complicated things with the pregnancy? That could be a huge stressor for his body, and I didn't want him under any more strain than necessary. Telling him I was a wolf shifter would definitely do that.

But I couldn't exactly keep it a secret forever. After all, our baby would be a shifter.

I needed to eliminate any anxiety for Bryce, especially now he was pregnant. However, I also had our child to think of. Things would be a hell of a lot easier if I could move everyone out to the homestead. I could take care of everything. I knew Bryce didn't like that there were things he couldn't do for Liam. I could do those things. Yes, Bryce was proud and wanted to do everything he could himself. He definitely wouldn't want me taking over, but I'd do everything in my power to do what I could. It was just a matter of telling him I was a shifter and moving him out there. Hah. Easier said than done.

I didn't have any answers by the time I pulled up in front of the lodge, so I headed straight back to my father's office. Thankfully, it was empty other than him.

"Jaxon! Another surprise visit?" He smiled as he turned from the window he'd been staring out of.

"Hey, Dad," I said with a small smile. "Guess I just know where to go when I need someone to talk to."

His smile faded slightly and he frowned. "Is everything okay?"

I sighed. Everything was wonderful. If I could just figure this out.

"I have some news for you. Maybe we should sit down. It's a big one."

He lifted an eyebrow. "Bigger than finding your fated mate?"

I smiled wryly. "Right on up there."

"Well, come on, then," he said, sitting on the couch. "Come talk to dear old Dad."

I already felt better. Greer Parsons wasn't just an excellent alpha pack leader. He was an amazing dad. Something I hoped I would be too. He'd always been there for me growing up, and I'd never been afraid to come to him with anything. I knew no matter what, he would love me and support me unconditionally. Still, I'd always worked my ass off to prove myself to him, wanting to be deserving of his approval, even though he gave it generously.

I thought again of our conversations about me becoming the pack leader when he stepped down. That was something he'd believed I could do, even when I hadn't. I knew deep down I didn't want to say no. I wanted to take on the challenge and prove he'd made the right choice entrusting that leadership to me. And for the first time, I was starting to think maybe I could. It was like fate had given me this chance to prove myself—to myself.

"Son?" My father's question pulled me out of my thoughts. Right.

"Bryce is pregnant," I said, going straight to the heart of the matter. No sense beating around the bush.

My dad's eyebrows flew up. "Well at least you get to the point. Wow!" He ran his hand over his face, his eyes wide as he processed that. Then a huge grin broke over his face.

I found myself smiling right back. "I know! It's crazy. I just found my mate, and now we're going to have a baby."

"I take it this is good news, then," he said, looking a little relieved. "I mean, I'm assuming you weren't planning on this just yet, but you seem happy."

"I'm ecstatic, Dad," I said frankly.

"And Bryce?"

I nodded. "He's thrilled too. Shocked, but excited nonetheless."

Dad looked at me sharply. "Have you told him…"

I sighed, shaking my head and leaning back on the couch. He got right to the point too, obviously realizing this was the real reason for my visit.

"Jaxon, you have to tell him."

"I know that. I do, and I was going to, just yesterday. But…" I told my dad what happened with Bryce yesterday, including the part about the wolf Bryce saw at the scene of the accident.

My dad blew out a rough breath at that. He didn't want to consider it could have been one of our shifters any more than I did. "Did he describe the wolf?"

"No, not really. I don't even know if he got that good of a look at it. Regardless, I don't think he'll take this well." I looked up at my dad, finally letting myself give in to some of the fear and darkness that had threatened all morning. "What do I do?"

What if he didn't want to be with me once he found out, is what I really meant. And Dad seemed to know that instinctively.

"You tell him. As soon as possible."

"But I'm worried about—"

"Jaxon."

My father's face turned stern. In alpha mode. "You can't move him onto the homestead until you tell him. Full stop. You know this."

Yeah. I did. I'd just hoped my dad would say something else. The thing was, I knew better. I nodded. "I know."

"Look," he said, a little softer now. "You love him. He loves you. He's excited about this baby. From what you've told me about him, he doesn't seem like the judgmental type. It will be a shock, no doubt—his whole worldview will have to shift, but if he loves you and sees you for the man you truly are—the strong, bold, caring man sitting in front of me right now—then you guys will work it out."

The words sounded good, but I still felt a pit of fear in my belly. I had to tell Bryce, and with a shifter baby on the way, I had to tell him soon. My chest constricted as I thought about how he could react. How this could ruin everything before it barely got started.

I left a little while later, my dad's parting words encouraging me to talk to Bryce.

I'd gotten the advice I was asking for. I would tell him. I just didn't know how—or when.

Chapter 14 - Bryce

We rode with the windows down all the way to Timberwood Cove General Hospital, and I felt as bright as the early June sun shining down on us.

Every day of the last two months had been better than the last—the best of my life—and today would be even better. We were headed in for our first well-baby checkup.

Jaxon had insisted we use his family doctor, that she was the best in the town, and that he wouldn't settle for anything less for his unborn child. It made me smile. He was so overprotective of me. Sometimes to an extreme, acting like I couldn't do anything for myself, but it only endeared him to me more.

Some days I still couldn't believe this was my life now. That I had this man who loved me so completely, who loved Liam and wanted us to be a family. We still hadn't moved in with Jaxon, despite what he'd said that morning when Liam asked, but maybe my earlier resistance had made him shy away.

As for any hesitations on my part, they were gone now. I knew Jaxon truly cared for us, and he meant it when he said he loved me.

"Liam was so mad he couldn't come," Jaxon said with a half-smile. "I felt bad for the little guy."

"He'll be okay," I replied. "I want this to be special. Just us. Besides, he's having a sleepover with Cole later anyway. That will make him forget all about it."

Jaxon chuckled, then rested his hand on my belly, like he did so often. Warmth filled me. I couldn't wait until I could feel the baby moving inside me. Jaxon would take up permanent residence next to me to feel it too, I was certain.

At the hospital, Jaxon stopped at the entrance. "Do you want me to get you a wheelchair?"

I laughed "Are you serious right now? I can absolutely walk into the hospital of my own accord."

He held his hands up in surrender, grinning. "Okay, okay. Can't blame me for wanting to take care of my mate."

There it was again. He said it from time to time. I mean, I felt like he was my soul mate too. I just found the expression a little odd.

"Well, at least get out here at the door so you don't have to walk across the parking lot."

I rolled my eyes, shaking my head. "Fine."

I climbed from the car, taking a couple steps before Jaxon called after me.

"Don't forget your cane!"

I turned back and grabbed it from where he was holding it out to me. "Thanks," I murmured then turned back and walked toward the sliding doors. That was something else that was odd. I'd felt exponentially less pain in my hips, legs and back over the past month or so. At times, like now, I felt like I might not even need my cane to walk. I still had a limp, but the pain wasn't nearly as severe. It barely impeded me on the best days.

The only thing I could think of was that being diligent with my physical therapy had paid off. I'd been told I'd suffer from the severe and sometimes debilitating pain for the rest of my life, even with the therapy. I mean, I was lucky to be walking at all, so I'd accepted that. Maybe I was just one of those exceptions, and that explained why I seemed to continue recovering better than expected. I probably shouldn't question it.

Jaxon jogged up beside me and planted a kiss on my lips, then slung his arm around my waist and led me into the hospital. "You ready for this?"

I smiled up at him. "Seriously can't wait."

He gave me a wink then strolled up to the reception desk and signed us in. When he sat down beside me and slipped an arm around my shoulders, I turned to study him. He had a self-assured grin on his face, his chest puffed out. I laughed. He'd been getting cockier lately, like the idea I was pregnant with his kid made him feel proud. It was adorable. Especially when I knew I was the one who got to see the softer side of him.

I'd noticed more and more how different he was with me over the time we'd been together. He had this strength and confidence about him whenever we were in public, but at home with me, he was just a big old softy. I loved it.

"What?" he asked, arching a brow.

I shook my head. "Nothing. Just wondering how you'll react to hearing the baby's heartbeat.

His eyes lit up like a kid on Christmas morning.

I didn't have to wait long to find out. A nurse ushered us back to a room, and then the doctor came in to see us in record time. Maybe having a friend of the family as our doctor wasn't a bad idea at all.

"Hi, I'm Dr. Reed," the woman said, introducing herself. "How are you feeling, Bryce?"

"Pretty good, actually," I said. "Nice to meet you."

"Maddie, how are you?" Jaxon asked, nodding at the doctor like they went way back.

She smiled. "How are you, is the question."

"Ridiculously attentive," I replied, giving Jaxon a pointed look. "He thought I needed a wheelchair just to come in here."

Dr. Reed laughed, her eyes shining. "Sounds about right. Okay, so who wants to hear this baby's heartbeat?"

She took a machine from beside the exam table and told me to lean back and pull up my shirt. After smearing my exposed skin with gel, she then pressed a gauge over my stomach. The next thing I knew, a racing beat was filling our ears. Strong and steady. And fast.

"Is it supposed to be that fast?" I asked, concern in my voice.

The doctor laughed. "Oh yes, that's a good sign. This baby sounds like a strong one, actually."

Jaxon smiled and laced his fingers through mine, and when I looked up at his face, I saw tears shining in his eyes. I squeezed his hand, tears saturating my own eyes. See, big old softy.

"That's our baby," I murmured to him, and when he looked at me, his gaze was full of wonder and love.

"Okay, let's check a few other things and then you can ask me all the questions you want," Dr. Reed said, interrupting our little moment. She got right through the exam seriously quickly, pronouncing at the end that dad and baby were both the picture of health. "Okay, what questions do you have?"

I reached into my pocket and pulled out a list. I was prepared. I had to be. After all, my disability could be a real issue. I had to be informed to make sure there wouldn't be any problems with the pregnancy, or my ability to care for the baby.

"That's what I'm here for," Jaxon reassured me. I knew he was, but I still wanted to make sure things were okay.

After getting the all clear from Dr. Reed and she'd answered my questions more than thoroughly, assuring me that caring for the baby shouldn't be any problem at all, we left the hospital.

Liam had spent the afternoon with a neighbor friend since we had the appointment, so we swung by to pick him up on the way home.

"Just grab your things and we'll take you right out to Cole's," I told him when we pulled in the driveway.

The whole ride out to Cole's house was full of questions from Liam, and we kept the windows down to enjoy the summer breeze. I looked out the window, realizing we were heading down the same road Jaxon had taken that day he'd shown me his house.

"I guess I didn't realize Linc lived out here by you," I commented. It made me realize just how little I actually knew about some parts of Jaxon's life. I'd met his father and been out to the homestead only that one time.

"Yeah, we all live out here," he said, and I thought I detected a hint of nervousness in his voice.

I wanted to press him for some answers, but not while Liam was in the car. After we dropped him off at Linc's, I'd expected we would go back to Jaxon's place since it was closer, but he just got back on the road heading back into town.

I turned to look at him, and saw tension in his shoulders, his jaw set firmly as he scanned the woods all around us. What was going on here? I wanted to ask, but the words died on my lips. My time with Jaxon since we'd found out about the baby had been nearly perfect, but there had been moments where my doubts crept in. This was one of them.

Jaxon said he wanted a relationship with me, but if that was the case, why wasn't he pushing me to move in with him like he had before? I mean, it was going on three months. Our relationship had grown so much since then. I loved him more than anything, and I wanted that future he'd painted a picture of. We were practically living together as it was. Jaxon slept with me every single night, so what was stopping him?

Maybe he was having his own doubts. What if he was just staying with me because of the baby, because of Liam and the promise to make sure the adoption went through?

I felt a sinking pit in my stomach. The adoption was only three days away. After that was taken care of, would Jaxon change his mind about us? Or had he already done so and just didn't want to come out and say it? Did he think I wasn't good enough for him? For his family and friends who were out at the homestead? I didn't know, and a million questions plagued my mind.

We rode in silence and I thought over the past couple months, trying to pinpoint if there was something I'd missed. In just about every scenario, Jaxon was absolutely perfect. Things just didn't add up, making me even more confused. As I thought about it, I became more and more worried, wondering if there was something Jaxon wasn't telling me.

There were also those random nights when Jaxon would just up and disappear for hours. He never said where he went, and he often waited until he thought I was asleep. What was that about?

Then there was the whole thing with his cock. How it would swell up so much when we had sex—to the point where it felt like we were stuck together. I didn't mention it much. After all, it was hard to complain when every time it happened I came harder than ever. But what if there was something wrong with him, something he needed to see a doctor about, just in case. Still, every time I had brought it up, he'd just dismissed it and said it was nothing.

With Jaxon tense beside me, his eyes still scanning the trees, I found it really hard to push away my fears. I'd been ignoring this for too long. It was something we needed to talk about because I needed to know where we really stood, especially since I had a baby to think of now.

But as we left the forest behind and the town opened up before us on the road, I noticed Jaxon visibly relaxing, the tension draining from his shoulders. His jaw released, and a smile started to creep over his face.

"I'm really looking forward to having the house all to ourselves," he murmured, glancing over at me, his grin widening.

I internally sighed, knowing I couldn't bring up my questions now. He looked so happy about the prospect of us having a whole night alone, and I didn't want to ruin it. Maybe that was weak of me, but I wanted to hang on to my hopes as long as possible, and I wanted this night with him as much as he apparently did.

By the time we got back to the house, the light in Jaxon's eyes had turned a bit darker, full of desire. He led me wordlessly into the house and straight to the bedroom. Then he pulled me into his arms and lowered his forehead to mine.

"How are you feeling?" he asked.

Confused. Conflicted. However, the elation at hearing our baby's heartbeat earlier made those emotions pale in significance. Plus there was the desire that sparked inside me every time Jaxon held me close and looked at me like I was the only man in the world. I let myself focus on that, wanting to forget everything else and just enjoy this moment with him.

"Hmm," I replied. "Like we better take advantage of this empty house for as long as we have it."

Jaxon chuckled, a glint in his eyes. "It's like you read my mind."

He lowered his lips to mine, backing me up until the backs of my thighs hit the bed. Taking his time, he kissed me with a barely restrained passion, exploring my mouth with his lips and my body with his hands.

I ran my hands up and over his chest, his shoulders, tangling my fingers in the ends of his hair while stroking the back of his neck with my thumbs. Jaxon arched his hips, grinding his cock against mine, already hard and throbbing and ready to go.

I groaned, my head falling back, and he trailed hot kisses down my jaw, my neck. Then he reached down and pulled my shirt up and over my head, tossing it aside. He kissed my chest, scraping his teeth across my nipples, and my body shivered in response.

"Jaxon." I pressed my cock harder against his, needing the friction. My cock was hard and swollen and begging for attention. My slick pooled around my hole, and Jaxon groaned.

"Fuck, you smell so good." He dropped to his knees in front of me and stripped me down until I was standing naked before him, my cock at full mast, bobbing in front of his face. He stuck his tongue out to gently lap at me, and my cock throbbed even harder.

"I'll be right back," he murmured, standing again and lowering me onto the bed.

For a moment, I worried he might just disappear again, but he was back less than a minute later, candles and a speaker in hand.

"I want tonight to be special," he said softly, his gaze tender, and my heart melted.

How could I doubt the way he felt about me when he treated me like I was the most precious thing he'd ever seen?

He moved around the room placing the candles and lighting them, then drawing the curtains so the room was only filled with the soft glow of candlelight. Then he set the speaker on the dresser and turned on soft music. When he looked back at me, his eyes were dark with lust, but his emotions were clear on his face.

He reached over his head and gripped his shirt between his shoulder blades then pulled it off. I licked my lips in anticipation, my body humming at the sight of his chiseled abs. His hair fell over his brow as he gave me a look that told me in no uncertain terms what he was going to do to me. I started to move toward him, but he shook his head slightly.

"Tonight is all about you."

My breath caught as he moved his hands to his belt, and I watched in growing eagerness as he stripped himself as bare as I was. Then he was climbing up on the bed, hovering over me.

He cupped my cheek with one hand, bracing himself with the other, and lowered his mouth to mine. His lips were soft, gentle, and he kissed me until my entire body was both completely relaxed and brimming with need.

He worked his way down my body, murmuring about how perfect I was. When he reached my belly, still mostly flat but showing the tiniest hints of a baby bump that would only be recognizable by the two of us, he caressed it softly before bestowing a sweet kiss. He whispered something to the baby—I didn't catch his words, though—and my heart melted even more. He loved this baby as much as I did, there was no doubt about it.

So why was I having doubts?

I gave myself over to the moment, focusing on the pure pleasure that shot through me when Jaxon kissed me even lower. His mouth trailed a wet line from my hip to the base of my cock, then up the throbbing shaft until he reached the tip. He flicked his tongue, and I cried out, my hips bucking.

I propped myself up on my elbows to watch him, and he gave me a wink, like he knew exactly what he was doing to me.

"Please, Jaxon," I begged when he trailed his fingers around my hip to squeeze my ass.

He continued licking and sucking my cock while he used his fingers to play with me, tracing circles around my hole, gathering my slick. My head fell back and I sucked in a sharp breath. Fuck, this felt so good. Like he was worshipping my body.

He took his time, working me up, building the sensations to a nearly unbearable height. When he finally sank his finger into my ass, I thought I might die of relief. Or come right then and there, since his mouth was now devouring my cock.

"Yes, Jaxon... Oh, god!" I cried out when he added another finger, thrusting deep inside my hole in slow, steady strokes. His head bobbed up and down on my cock, his eyes on mine the entire time. I felt my balls tighten and tried to warn him that I was about to come, but he seemed to sense it instinctively and pulled out.

Lifting his head, he smirked. "Feeling good?"

I gasped, barely coherent as my body burned with the white-hot fire that was pulsing through my veins.

He chuckled lightly, then sat back on his knees. Slinging my legs over his shoulders, he positioned his cock so the wide tip pressed gently against my entrance.

I couldn't look away as he slowly slid into me. The muscle in his jaw tightened, like he was fighting to restrain himself, and when he finally bottomed out his mouth fell open on a soft gasp and his eyelids fluttered closed.

I clenched my ass around him, drawing a guttural moan from his throat. Then his gaze snapped back to mine as he began to move inside of me. Slow, long, languorous strokes. All the way in, then pulling out until just the tip of him remained inside me. Over and over, he fucked me, gently, sweetly. Passionately.

He meant it when he said tonight was all about me. Because he was doing everything he could to draw out every ounce of pleasure in my body. The way he was looking at me was enough to make my heart skip a beat. So tenderly. Adoringly. Like this was everything to him. I understood because I felt the same way.

When we were both straining to hang on to the last bit of sanity, our bodies sweaty, our breaths coming in ragged gasps, Jaxon pushed my knees up and came down between my legs to capture my mouth in a kiss. This was more urgent. Searing.

Then he was moving faster inside me, racing toward his release. He reached between us, wrapping his fist around my cock, and began to stroke me hard, matching the rhythm of his thrusts.

We both fell over the edge together, our orgasms rocketing through us. Claiming us. I clung to him, kissing him with everything I had in me. Memorizing this moment because I knew then that no matter what doubts I may have, none of them mattered. All that mattered was the love we shared for each other and Liam and the life growing inside me.

And there was nothing that could take that away from us.

Chapter 15 - Jaxon

"Cole's room is so cool," Liam enthused from the passenger seat of my car. We were on the way to Saturday afternoon practice.

"I take it you had fun last night, then?" I asked with a grin. As usual, he was bouncing on the seat in excitement.

"Yeah! He showed me all this wolf stuff he has all over his house. It was the coolest."

"Like a collection?" I asked, though I knew what he was talking about. Shit. What had he seen out there? My suspicions were confirmed with his next words.

"Cole said he was a wolf shifter. You know, like the urban legends of werewolves or something. I have heard stories since we moved here."

I glanced at him. Great. So Cole had talked about it. He knew he wasn't supposed to, but at the same time, he also probably knew from Linc that I was wanting to move them both out to the homestead. He may have even assumed Liam already knew.

It made me realize I needed to talk to Bryce as soon as possible. The more Liam hung around Cole, the more he'd learn. The secrets would all be out there. I didn't need Bryce or Liam learning about shifters from anyone but me.

"What kind of stories?" I asked cautiously.

He shrugged. "Just that there are people who turn into wolves out in the woods near where Cole lives. I think Cole was just pulling my leg about being a shifter, though," he added with a laugh.

"What do you think about those stories?" I asked, trying to keep my voice light.

He shrugged again, though he was grinning now. "I think it would be cool if they were true. It would be awesome to be a wolf shifter!"

"You'd like that, huh?" I couldn't help asking, feeling excited about the prospect of claiming him and Bryce and making them shifters as well.

"Totally!"

I smiled, not saying anything else, but it made it clear to me I had to tell Bryce—tonight. Not only because I couldn't risk him finding out through Liam, but also because I'd just confirmed some suspicions I had when I'd been out at the lodge.

I talked to the elders about how Bryce seemed to be improving day by day as far as his disability went. He was walking better, usually without a cane, and if I didn't know he had a limp I might not have even noticed it. It was the baby. Its shifter blood was affecting Bryce's body. Wolf DNA was even more potent than I realized. The elders had then told me that a claiming bite would heal him completely.

Needless to say, the idea of claiming my mate held even more appeal now. I'd been so worried about telling him, that it would ruin our relationship after he found out about wolf shifters, especially in light of what happened with his sister. Now I felt more confident about the decision. I didn't know what that would mean for our relationship going forward—I still had a niggling worry in the back of my mind—but I had to hope for the best because our future seemed nothing short of perfect.

Once we got to practice, I sent the kids out onto the field to warm up, then motioned Linc to come over away from earshot.

"We could have a problem," I muttered.

Linc frowned. "What's up?"

I told him all about how Cole had leaked confidential information about shifters that could hurt the pack. Not that we would have anything to worry about once I came out to Bryce, but if Cole was talking this loosely, we had to make sure he knew it wasn't okay.

"It put the entire shifter community at risk of exposure. You have to talk to him."

"Spoken like a true pack leader," Linc said with a grin.

"I'm serious, Linc." I frowned at him.

Holding his hands up, he said, "I know, I know, and I understand the gravity of this. I'll give Cole a good talking to." He grinned again. "But seriously, you sounded just like an alpha leader right then. Can I take this to mean you're ready to take over the pack?"

That was another thing I'd finally solidified in my mind.

"I am." I nodded firmly. "Actually, it's Bryce who made me feel this way. Taking care of him has shown me I do have what it takes to look after people who aren't always capable of looking after themselves. And I realized that's pretty much the essence of being a pack leader. Taking care of what's yours and protecting them at all costs."

Linc smiled wider and clapped me on the shoulder. "I knew you'd finally come around to seeing what the rest of us have known all along. Congratulations, man."

I grinned back, thinking about the future ahead of me. I'd have my pack to lead, my mate by my side as a shifter, our son and baby on the way. I'd put off making this happen for too long.

Tonight, that would change.

***

The scent of lasagna hit my nose as soon as Liam and I walked into the house.

"Honey, I'm home," I called out as Liam darted into the kitchen. I followed him and found Bryce standing in the kitchen in an apron, a tray of garlic bread in one hand.

He grinned. "I wanted to surprise you guys with a nice dinner."

"Mission accomplished," I said, crossing to him to give him a kiss. "Looks like you're moving around well today."

Bryce nodded. "Yeah. Honestly, it feels almost like I'm getting better and better with each day that passes. It's almost like magic. I don't understand it, but I'm not complaining," he said with a smile.

A thrill raced through me thinking about how he might feel when he found out he would be healed completely when he became a shifter. I thought about the conversation ahead of me all through dinner—the lasagna was delicious, and he'd even made some cannelloni from scratch. By the time it was Liam's bedtime, I was full of nervous anticipation.

Bryce and I tucked him in together—as we did most night now—sitting down on each side of his bed.

"I want to be a wolf shifter like Cole," he proclaimed without preamble.

I blinked a couple times, but before I could figure out what to say, Bryce was laughing and reaching up to brush a strand of hair off Liam's forehead.

"I've told you time and time again that shifters are just a myth. A conspiracy. They don't really exist," he said gently, and my stomach clenched. Talk about an unexpected lead in to the conversation we needed to have.

Yes, actually, Bryce, wolf shifters are real indeed. And surprise! I am one!

I had no idea how this would go over now. What if he thought I was crazy?

"Yes, they are!" Liam protested. "Me and Cole saw a man turn into a wolf last night when I spent the night there."

Bryce laughed, shaking his head. "You were obviously half-asleep and dreaming."

My stomach felt like a ball of ice had settled there, and I barely contained the fury that was boiling through me. Shit! How could I have let this happen? I shouldn't have let Liam go out there. Or more to the point, I shouldn't have let this go on so long without telling Bryce the truth.

That knowledge hit me hard, and I was suddenly terrified. Fighting to keep a calm face, I smiled at Liam. "Speaking of dreaming, I think it's about time you caught some shut-eye, buddy."

Bryce agreed, and we got Liam tucked in before heading out of his room. I went to clean up the kitchen, gathering my thoughts, while Bryce said he was going to take a bath. I had to tell him tonight, there was no doubt about that. I just had to get it right. I didn't want to scare him.

When I finished up in the kitchen, I went to check on Liam. Finding him sound asleep, I knew now was the time. I couldn't put this off any longer.

Bryce was just coming out of the bathroom, a towel slung low around his hips. As I backed up to his bedroom he stepped toward me, still dripping wet, a mischievous glint in his eyes. I groaned internally. I knew that look. Bryce wanted me—bad, and now; his pregnancy hormones seemingly making him extra horny.

When he closed the last of the space between us and reached straight for my cock, I found myself already responding to him. Fuck. I really needed to talk to him.

He squeezed my shaft through my pants, and all thoughts of conversation went right out of my head. *Later*. I'd do it later because how could I resist the sexiness that was my mate, practically begging to be fucked? I growled, my wolf close to the surface. Thinking about making Bryce my mate apparently had him ready to go. I yanked Bryce toward me, his towel falling to the floor. His cock bobbed in front of me, long and hard, and I grabbed his hips, grinding myself against him.

"You want this?"

He groaned. "Pretty sure you do too."

I grinned then crushed my mouth to his, sweeping inside. He dove his fingers into my hair, and we were a clash of lips and teeth and tongues. My wolf howled, longing to reach out to his mate. To bite him. To claim him.

I scraped my teeth over Bryce's neck, feeling his pulse beat strong and fast. The urge to claim him now was nearly overwhelming. So far I'd been able to keep it at bay, but right now, knowing I was so close to having everything finally fall into place, I could barely resist.

I jerked myself away from him with another growl, then spun him around, pushing him forward toward the dresser. He gripped the wood tightly, shoving his hips back, teasing my cock while his begging moans filled my ears. It was a good thing he was already slick because I couldn't hold back. I felt primal, raw. Desperate for all of him. If I couldn't claim my mate right now, I'd sure fuck him with everything I had.

His cries echoed off the walls as I slammed into him, burying myself fully in his tight ass.

"Fuck, Bryce," I ground out, already feeling my knot starting to form. God, he was driving me crazy tonight. My wolf was barely contained, and I felt savage as I took Bryce's ass over and over. He mumbled incoherently, every thrust eliciting another cry. His body vibrated beneath me, his walls convulsing. My knot began to swell even more as I fucked him hard.

I looked up, catching sight of us in the mirror over the dresser, almost surprised by the feral look in my eyes. Bryce looked sexy as hell, his hair falling over his face, his pupils blown out, nearly black with desire as he met my gaze. His mouth fell open in pleasure, then he gasped for breath and whispered my name.

And I was done. I came with a vengeance, a full-body orgasm that had me crying out my release. I erupted inside my mate, my cock locked in his ass, the knot intensifying the pleasure for both of us.

Bryce clamped down even tighter on my cock, and I reached around him to grip his rock-hard length. Then he was coming too, giant convulsions wracking his body as he poured out warm cum all over my hand.

My body felt like liquid as I wrapped my arms around Bryce, holding him up. I moved us to the bed, and we both fell onto it, barely able to breathe.

"Holy shit."

"Yeah," I grunted. "Tell me about it."

Bryce rolled to his side and looked at me. "What's happening when you do that?" he asked.

I knew he was referring to my knot. He'd asked about it enough already, more so lately. I couldn't just brush it off again. Not after that, when I'd felt so savage, ready to claim him right then and there. I had to tell him. Everything.

I stared at the ceiling, gathering my thoughts. Not easy when my brain was still addled from sex. He waited. He didn't want to hear an excuse this time either. It felt like there was something heavier about this moment. Like he'd known there was something I wasn't telling him, and he wasn't going to let it go any longer.

Good thing I'd come to the same conclusion.

"I have to tell you something," I said. I risked a glance at him, seeing surprise on his face, but also relief. It gave me the courage to go on. I sat up on the bed, and Bryce followed suit, facing me.

I took his hands in mine. "I don't want there to be any secrets between us, but I have been keeping something from you."

He nodded silently.

I took a deep breath, ready to bare my soul. But I wasn't afraid anymore. What I truly felt was proud. Proud of who and what I was. That was something that had been hard-won, but I'd realized after finding Bryce that I was capable of being both a good mate and a good alpha for the pack. He'd helped me move past my self-doubt, whether he knew it or not. He deserved to know the truth now.

"That man who Liam saw in the woods at the homestead," I said, seeing confusion in Bryce's eyes at where I was going with this. "The wolf shifter. Liam didn't dream that. He saw it with his own eyes."

Bryce stared at me, then he scoffed and shook his head. "Jaxon, what the hell are you talking about?"

I blew out a breath. "Wolf shifters are real, Bryce. I know because I am one. That's what I haven't been telling you. That's why my cock swells up when we have sex—it's called a knot, and it happens in alpha shifters."

His eyes darted down to my cock, at half-mast now, the knot gone. When he looked back up at me, he looked wary. I had to keep going. Let him see what wonderful news this was.

"And you, Bryce. You're my fated mate. In the shifter world, that's everything. When a shifter claims a mate, it's for life. To have found you... It's more than I ever could have hoped for. I love you so much and I'm so happy you're my mate. I can't wait to claim you and make you mine forever."

His eyes narrowed, his back straightening as he continued to stare at me. To say he was shocked was an understatement, but what I hadn't seen coming was the dismay that was also beginning to show.

Determined to show him how amazing this would be, I gripped his arms. "Bryce. I've also learned from the pack elders that a claiming bite will heal you. It will turn you into a wolf shifter, and your new DNA will heal all of your existing ailments. It's why you've been walking better." I set my palm on his stomach. "It's because you have my baby in here. A shifter, and its blood is already helping you. Don't you see, Bryce? We'll all be able to move out to the homestead with the rest of the pack. I'm supposed to be the next pack leader, but I haven't felt ready. Until you. I know now I am ready, but only if I have you by my side."

I was rambling now, trying to get it all out there. Trying to fill the empty air of Bryce's shock with something...anything, since he wasn't responding.

He looked down at my hand on his stomach, then jerked his head back up, horror written all over his face.

Oh god.

He thought I was crazy. He didn't believe me. He thought I had in fact been keeping a secret—that I was delusional.

"I'll show you," I said, jumping from the bed.

Bryce couldn't have looked any more terrified. Or so I thought. Until I shifted.

My perception changed as I let my wolf take over. Smell became more pronounced, sight grayed out a little, but I always felt stronger, more powerful in my wolf form. I shook out my coat and stretched, opening my jaws wide to accommodate my newly erupted canines.

Bryce screamed.

I took a step toward him, but he backed up on the bed, so I stopped. I wanted nothing more than to go to him, to nuzzle up against him and show him it was okay, that everything would be okay. But the look on his face kept me frozen in place.

Liam's door flung open, and he came running in, obviously awakened by all the noise. His gaze landed on me and his eyes went comically wide before he broke out in a huge grin.

Liam ran toward me. "Jaxon?" He came to a stop right in front of me.

"Liam, get back," Bryce commanded, and my wolf whined, already feeling a connection to Liam; accepting him and loving him, wanting to claim him as family. The idea that Liam might be scared of my wolf was like being pierced in the heart.

But I didn't have to worry. Liam came right up to me, resting his hand on my muzzle. I sniffed at him, then licked his fingers with my tongue. He laughed, his eyes full of wonder, then he flung his arms around my neck. He wasn't afraid at all.

I nuzzled his head and looked at Bryce over Liam's shoulder. Bryce looked like he didn't know what to think about this, his expression shifting from horror to...pissed.

Shit.

I quickly pulled away from Liam and shifted back to human form. I reached for Bryce's fallen towel to cover myself. Bryce had already found a blanket to wrap around him.

"Bryce..." I tried to think of something to say that would fix this, but when I locked eyes with him again I realized nothing was going to fix how fucked I was because pissed didn't even *begin* to describe Bryce.

He was absolutely livid.

Chapter 16 - Bryce

It felt like I'd fallen through a glass mirror and tumbled out on the other side into an alternate reality. Ones in which things of fairy tales were true. Sure, I'd heard the stories about the Timberwood Cove wolves, but I'd never believed any of it. It was just an urban legend.

Now I couldn't deny what I'd seen. Jaxon had turned into a wolf right here in front of me, and now he was telling me all kinds of crazy things about being mates, being the leader of a pack, about how he thought I could become a shifter too and be healed from my injuries.

I shook my head. None of that made any sense at all. But as the pieces of what he was saying started to come together they formed a new picture, something I never imagined, but was now becoming clear.

I looked down at my stomach, and another wave of shock hit me, accompanied by a flash of dread. This baby was a wolf shifter. I was carrying a wolf pup inside me. The child of the future pack leader. On its own, it was a lot to process, and I could see Jaxon was hoping I'd accept what he was telling me, but just then another image flashed through my mind. A wolf in the middle of the road. Bright green eyes shining in my headlights.

There were times when I'd thought maybe I'd seen a dog out there in the road the night Lorelei died. Not a wolf—because a *wolf*? That was crazy, right? But now I knew the truth. It *had* been a wolf, and not of the wild variety. A shifter. Most likely from Jaxon's pack.

Anger surged through me, warring with the pain of my heart crumbling.

I stood from the bed. "You need to go." I was surprised at how calm I sounded, though my tone was deathly cold.

"Bryce..." Jaxon took a step toward me, but I threw my hands up.

It was all too much to take in. I didn't know what to think. What to feel. I needed some space to process.

"Just leave, Jaxon," I repeated, more forcefully this time.

"No, we need to talk about this."

I noticed a movement in the corner of my eye, and remembered Liam was still standing here, his eyes now wide and terrified. "Go to your room, Liam."

My tone left no room for argument, and though it hurt to talk to Liam like that, I needed him safe, away from Jaxon.

When Jaxon and I were alone again, I turned on him. "You should have told me. You should have been honest with me. How could you not have said anything all this time? You should have told me from the very beginning, Jaxon."

"Bryce, please," he said, his expression pained. "Let me explain. Please, don't push me away right now. We need to talk about this."

"I don't want to talk to you right now." My voice vibrated with barely suppressed anger. "You've lied to me. You've put Liam in danger, having him around dangerous animals and not letting me in on the fact. You've put me in danger! Why would I want to hear what you have to say when everything has been a lie from the very beginning?"

"It's not been a lie," he said, his eyes full of longing. "I love you, Bryce. Everything I've ever said has been the truth."

"It's what you *didn't* say! That's the problem. A wolf, Jaxon? A wolf! It was a fucking wolf that caused the death of my sister!" I was shouting by the time I was finished.

I couldn't help it. The pain of this betrayal fueled my anger. "Go. Now. I don't want to have anything to do with wolves. Not now. Not ever."

"Bryce, please." Jaxon took another step toward me, and I instinctively backed up. He stopped. "Bryce, my pack isn't dangerous. My wolf isn't dangerous. Please, don't send me away now. Let me explain. I love you, more than anything."

I pointed at the door, my hand shaking with rage. "Get OUT!"

The force of my shout seemed to knock Jaxon back a step. He blinked a couple times, grief cutting across his face. He shook his head, but he didn't come closer. I couldn't tell if he thought I was afraid of him or if he was afraid of pushing me too far.

Either way, he finally did as I asked. He swallowed hard and nodded, then began gathering his clothes and yanking them on.

I stood there like I was carved from stone, my expression carefully blank, my body stiff. I didn't so much as want to breathe him in, afraid I would second guess myself. But I needed time to process this. Alone.

With one last lingering look, his green eyes sorrowful, Jaxon headed toward the door. Then he turned. "This isn't over, Bryce. I love you."

I watched his retreating back, feeling the truth of both statements. He did love me. It should have made me feel better, but it didn't. This was far from over and I had no idea how to handle it. It couldn't be over because I was carrying Jaxon's child. His pup.

I rested my hand on my stomach, trying to make sense of it all. Trying to reconcile my mind to this entirely new viewpoint, this new world I was suddenly living in. I jumped when I heard the front door slam.

Then Liam was running back in my room, tears coursing down his red face.

"How—how could you? How could you...send...him...away?" His words stuttered and broke with the strength of the sobs that wracked his body.

I immediately went to him, wrapping him in my arms, but he pushed back and looked up at me. His hazel eyes were full of hurt and anger. Echoing how I was feeling. Only his was directed at me.

"Liam... I just." I blew out a breath and raked a hand through my hair. "I'm just trying to make sense of this. Shifters existing. Jaxon being one. All of it."

"I wanted to move to the homestead. I wanted us to be a family. I wanted to be part of their pack. I feel safe there. They can take care of us. Give us what we need to stay together. And you made him leave," he said accusingly.

His words cut deep, and my heart ached even more. I didn't want him to feel like he wasn't safe with me, but it wasn't just that. Liam was attached to Jaxon. He adored him and looked up to him, and to be honest, Jaxon was good for Liam. Jaxon had been good for both of us.

But now what? Liam wasn't wrong. Being with Jaxon would practically ensure Liam's adoption, which was only a couple of days away. What was I supposed to do without Jaxon? The thought terrified me on a multitude of levels. I couldn't imagine my life without him, and I wasn't sure I could succeed with the adoption case on my own.

"I don't know what's going to happen," I finally responded, trying to be as truthful as the situation allowed. I honestly had no idea what the future held.

Liam gripped my hands, a hopeful gleam purging some of his anger. "Please, Uncle Bryce, don't give up on him. Jaxon is amazing, and I know you love him. Don't be afraid of the shifters."

God, this kid. He desperately wanted me to change my mind and keep Jaxon in our lives.

"I can't make any promises, Liam."

His hope veered back to anger, his brows drawing together, then he turned and stormed from the room. I could hear him a few seconds later sobbing into his pillow.

I felt like the biggest piece of shit ever. A total failure. I was completely clueless about what to do, how to find my way through this crazy mess my life had become. I'd hurt Liam, and no doubt I'd hurt Jaxon.

What if by sending Jaxon away I'd set myself up to lose everything that meant the most to me?

Tears pricked my eyes, and my throat stung. I crawled back on my bed and let the tears come, giving into the pain, crying until there was nothing left inside but a resounding ache in an otherwise hollow chest.

Chapter 17 - Jaxon

I barely remembered the drive home.

I don't want to be with a wolf. Not now, not ever…

Bryce's words echoed in my mind over and over, drowning out everything except a piercing heartache, my pain and anger amplified by my wolf mourning the loss of its mate.

By the time I burst through my front door, my wolf was clawing to be let free. I strode through the house and out the backdoor, and then with a vicious growl, I unleashed the beast inside me, giving him full control.

And we ran.

I headed deep into the thick forest that backed up to my house at the edge of the pack homestead. I pushed myself until my lungs burned and my muscles protested, and then I pushed myself harder. Anything to try to dull the sound of Bryce's voice, the look on his face.

I'd caused that look of horror and anguish, all because I'd failed to tell him sooner.

No, not just that…

The little voice in my head kept me from losing myself totally in my wolf. I wanted to escape from the pain. To feel nothing but the crisp evening air on my face, to smell the scent of underbrush and earth mixing with the leaves and wildflowers, to hear the forest creatures and distant water and pounding of my feet as I ran.

But that little voice wouldn't let me have that peace. Not when there was more behind Bryce's ultimatum. He was afraid of me. He'd made it clear he wanted nothing to do with wolves. That was the worst part; thinking he might be unable to love me for who I was at my core—a shifter.

I don't want to be with a wolf. Not now, not ever…

My wolf howled in protest, the sound echoing through the night, rising up above the trees and into the blackness of the sky. The idea of not being with my mate was unacceptable.

There had to be a way I could sort this out. Something. Somehow. I wouldn't let this be the end. I'd told him as much, and I meant it. Resolve welled up in my chest, not alleviating my torment, but at least I no longer felt as if my world was coming to an end.

I had to get him to change his mind about everything, to understand I was still the same man he fell in love with, that he didn't have to be afraid of my wolf. That we belonged together.

My wolf howled again, longing for his mate.

I'll fix this, I vowed. *No matter what it takes.*

I continued to run through the forest, my plan falling into place. By the time I got back to my house over an hour later, there was only one missing piece, and I knew just the person to talk to about it.

***

I stood in my father's office just past the crack of dawn. I'd barely been able to wait until morning to request the meeting with him, and he'd shown up right away.

"What's going on, Jaxon?" he asked as came into the office. His hair was still rumpled, and he'd thrown on an old t-shirt and jeans, like he'd jumped straight of bed to come right over and meet me.

A smile tipped my lips. My dad was someone you could count on to come to your aid at the drop of a hat, no matter the time of day. It's part of what made him such a great leader.

I realized it was something I saw in myself too. Being with Bryce really had shown me I had what it took to take care of other people too. Suddenly, I was struck with a thought. Ever since Bryce had come into my life I'd had him to focus on, to take care of. Not once had I felt myself slipping into my old self-deprecating thought patterns. I used to replay my failures nearly daily. I'd told myself for so long I didn't have what it takes to be a champion ball player, to find my mate, to lead the pack.

On my run last night when I'd refused to accept defeat, I also realized I'd let go of the fear of failing others. I didn't know exactly when it happened, but certainly over the course of the last three months I'd found who I was meant to be. And I was ready to fulfill my promise as an alpha to my mate—and as a leader to my pack.

I stepped toward my father now, confidence mounting. "Dad. I'm ready to take over as pack leader."

He blinked only for a second before a wide grin spread across his face. "I knew you'd figure it out soon enough, son. I just wish you hadn't chosen six in the morning to tell me about it."

I nodded. "That's because that's not all I need to talk to you about."

"Let me get some coffee then," he said with nod of his own. "You want some?"

"Yeah, that'd be great." I claimed a chair in the sitting area then leaned forward to steeple my fingers together.

"You look like you're already the pack leader, son," Dad said, as he came back over and handed me a mug of coffee.

"Well, then let's get right down to business."

If he looked surprised at my commanding tone, he didn't show it, unless the grin counted. Standing there in his casual clothes with his hair rumpled, that youthful grin on his face, my dad almost looked like he could be my older brother. He bore the weight of leading a pack well, and definitely didn't look like someone who was old enough to retire.

"I told you about the accident Bryce was involved in, that he said he saw a wolf in the middle of the road and swerved to avoid it. Well, I need to know if it could have been anyone from the Timberwood Cove pack." That was the first step.

He shook his head slowly. "I don't see how it could be. You know for sure it was a shifter?"

"I told Bryce the truth last night." I quickly gave my dad the short version of the story, bringing him up to speed with what happened and Bryce's reaction, including the part about him more or less blaming the wolf for his sister's death. "I just have to be sure it wasn't one of ours."

"Absolutely," my dad said. "But I can tell you that if it had been anyone from our pack, we'd know. They would have reported causing an accident like that."

I didn't doubt it. Dad trusted his pack implicitly, and for good reason. They looked up to him and trusted him too. It was something I intended to do as well.

"Okay," I said. "If we're certain, then I need you to call an emergency initiation ceremony and make me the pack leader tonight."

"Whoa, hang on." He laughed, holding his hands up. "What's the rush? I mean, I know you're ready..."

"I have to fix things with Bryce. As soon as possible, and the only way to do that is to prove to him that wolves aren't dangerous, which is what he thinks. He needs to see how our pack is—that we're like family, and he can trust us. I want him to see us as a united front, to see he doesn't have anything to fear. That we'll all welcome him in as part of the pack."

He gave me a sympathetic smile and reached out to squeeze my shoulder. It wasn't pity, though. He just wanted me to know he was there for me. "You know the whole pack will stand behind you in whatever you need. You have something in mind, don't you?"

My father knew me so well. "Yes. And that's why I need to go through with this initiation tonight. Liam's adoption hearing is tomorrow morning. I want to be there for him, the pack standing beside me. I want us to all speak on Bryce's behalf and prove to the judge that Bryce and Liam will be well taken care of, no matter what. That we're like family. More than that I want to show Bryce it will all be okay."

"You're going to make a fine mate, Jaxon," Dad said, then he stood and clapped his hands together. "I'll get on it right and let the pack know there's an emergency gathering."

"I'll help," I said, diving right in and working alongside my father.

***

We stood under the auspiciously full moon at eleven o'clock that night. The air was heavy, thick with the summer rain that had fallen that afternoon. The smell of damp earth mingled with floral hints on the cool breeze.

The entire pack was here, from the elders to children—except those who were too young to go on a pack run. I stood on the wide circular platform near the edge of the pond. A light mist rose from the surface, warmed from the summer sun and cooled by the crisp night air. My gaze traced the ragged perimeter of the centuries-old stone, worn from being exposed to the elements for who knew how long. This is where every pack leader of the Timberwood Cove pack had been initiated for as far back as our history went.

And now I was standing here. In front of the pack that would be mine in a matter of moments. The pack gathered in a semi-circle around the platform, the elders in the front. To my side was my father. The alpha of the pack I'd grown up in. The man who'd raised me to be who I'd become.

He smiled at me, pride radiating from him. We were dressed pretty informally since the emergency ceremony was so last-minute. Normally, there would be a huge celebration, a party where the entire pack could get together after the traditional pack run that followed the initiation. There were usually a lot of traditions and ceremonies to adhere to, but we didn't have time to prepare for all of it, and I didn't particularly have the patience right now. I just wanted to simply step into my role. We couldn't completely ignore all tradition, though.

"Wolves of the Timberwood Cove pack, we thank you tonight for being part of this momentous occasion."

I arched my eyebrow at my father. *Really?* But my father loved tradition. It showed how much he cared for me that he would circumvent the normal ceremony so I could be there with my pack for Bryce by morning.

His eyes crinkled around the edges, then he stepped forward and gave a short but inspiring speech about his faith in me, their new alpha. He stepped back and turned to face me. I'd never felt more blessed to have him look at me the way he did—full of confidence and love. Then he lifted his hand.

In his fingers he held the ring that signified the position of pack alpha. Yellow gold etched with black formed a wide band that encased a large circular stone. Moonstone.

"I believe this is yours now," he said. The pack was silent as he handed it to me, the significance of the moment signaling the transfer of leadership.

Then it was on my finger. My chest swelled with pride, and I stepped forward, holding my fist to my heart.

"Timberwood Cove wolves," I said, my voice strong and steady, like that of a leader. "I'm honored and humbled to be your alpha. I swear I will fulfill my duties to you—my family, my packmates—with everything I have in me. It's a privilege to be your leader."

A roar of cheers greeted my statement, and I felt my father sling and arm around my shoulder.

"Time to lead your pack on a run, son." I could have sworn I saw a tear in the corner of his eye.

He stepped to the side again, and I shifted. This time, though, I was somehow larger than I'd been before, standing taller and more commanding. The new alpha.

I stretched and then tipped my head to the moon. Howling, I signaled the next tradition, the ceremonial shifting, which only happened on special occasions, such as a claiming ceremony. When we normally shifted as a pack we didn't stand on ceremony, but this was one of those times.

Traditionally, as the lead alpha I would always shift first. Then usually came the elders. However, as my father had just stepped down from pack alpha, he had the right to shift next, though in future he would shift with the rest of the elders. Once my father was standing to my side and slightly back on the platform, the elders took their wolf form. Finally, the rest of the pack shifted.

I howled at the moon once more, and this time the rest of my pack responded in kind. Our howls reverberated through the night. Then we ran.

I took the lead, running straight into the tree line. The pack followed behind in the same order as they'd shifted, but once we were well into the woods, we fanned out and went our own way, breaking off into smaller groups.

As I ran, my mind went to Bryce. I couldn't wait to have him running beside me one day, and I was determined to make it happen. I would get him back, and we'd have everything we ever wanted. Finally, everything would be alright.

Chapter 18 - Bryce

Today was going to be one of the hardest days of my life, ranking right up there with the night Lorelei died. Yesterday had been difficult enough, knowing I very well may have ruined the best thing that had ever happened to me by pushing Jaxon away.

But it was nothing compared to the idea of facing what was ahead of me without Jaxon by my side, supporting me through the adoption hearing. It was set for ten o'clock this morning.

I was up at the crack of dawn trying to prepare myself for it. Physically, I felt better than I had in a long time, every day that passed improving my condition. I knew now it was because of the shifter DNA coursing through my blood. From the baby I carried inside me. Jaxon's baby.

I tried to draw on that physical strength, but it wasn't helping me with my emotional state. I was a complete mess. Liam's future was at stake, and I didn't know what to expect. I had to hope Mrs. Pinder was still on my side. She didn't know the details of what had happened with Jaxon. As far as she knew, we were still a couple. Would it be enough, though?

By the time Liam woke and came into the kitchen where I was preparing breakfast, I was a jumble of nerves.

"Morning, big man," I said, giving him a cheerful smile. "You ready for this?"

He looked at me, nerves shining in his own eyes. He shrugged wordlessly and sat down at the table. I drew in a deep breath and brought him his eggs and pancakes, then sat down beside him.

"It's going to be okay, Liam. Don't worry."

But I wasn't sure my assurances were encouragement enough. He'd been nearly as miserable as I was after I'd sent Jaxon away. Liam was upset with me, I knew that much, but I also knew he was worried about how the adoption hearing would go without Jaxon there with us.

When he finally spoke, his words nearly crushed me. "Can we go visit Mom before going to the courthouse?"

My heart thudded painfully. I thought what I was going through was bad, but I couldn't imagine how scary all of this must be for him. All the uncertainty. He'd been through so much already, and the possibility that he might not be able to stay with me weighed heavy on both of us.

"Of course," I replied, pulling myself together. I had to be strong for his sake.

Thirty minutes later, we were in the cemetery, Lori's gravestone before us. Liam had insisted we stop at the store for fresh flowers. He clutched them tightly as he bent down in front of the grave.

"Hey, Mom," he said softly, his voice wavering. Hearing him so forlorn, I almost cried. No child should have to endure what Liam had.

Determination settled in my body. I would do everything in my power to make sure I got to keep him. He needed me. I needed him. We were family, and he was as much a part of me now as the baby growing inside me. A son in every way that mattered.

"Today's a pretty big day," he continued, brushing some of the dirt and grass from the headstone before replacing the old flowers with the vibrant wash of color from the summer bouquet he'd picked out. "I need you with us. Bryce needs you with us. Please help us..."

His voice cracked, and he collapsed onto the ground, clutching the grass. Sobs tore through his little body. I'd never seen him break down like this. He'd stayed strong even through her funeral, but his desperation was clear right now. Everything he knew could be ripped out from under him.

I clenched my fists. Surely the judge would see we belonged together, that family meant everything. I was the last family Liam had. The judge had to recognize that remaining in my care was the best thing for him.

I wished Jaxon was with us. He'd provide the strength and comfort Liam and I both needed if he were standing beside us now. But I'd ruined that. In my anger and pain I'd pushed him away. Was it too late? Was there any hope of fixing things between us?

I shoved aside the thoughts and my own self-pity. I didn't have time to think about that today. I had to focus entirely on Liam and seeing him through this. I had to be his rock in Jaxon's stead.

"Please, Mom," Liam said, still weeping. "Please make sure I don't have to go to foster care."

My heart breaking, I knelt down beside him. I found it surprisingly easy, not even needing my cane. If only everything else about today were that effortless…

"Come here, Liam," I said, pulling him to me.

He turned in my arms, burying his face in my shirt, clinging to me as he continued to cry.

"I'm so scared, Uncle Bryce," he whispered tremulously.

"Shh." I rubbed his back. "It's going to be okay."

"Why did you make Jaxon leave?" he asked, lifting his tear-stained face to look at me. There was no anger there this time. Just confusion. "He made everything so much easier for us. So much better. We need him, Uncle Bryce."

We did indeed, but right now I didn't know where we stood. I had to face this alone.

"I know, Liam." I sighed heavily.

"Then take him back. Please!" His eyes glittered, entreaty shining through his tears. "Think about how much he's helped us. We could be a family, just like he said. You and me and Jaxon and the baby."

Liam rested his hand on my stomach, and I could have sworn I felt a little flutter deep in my belly. Every day I was feeling more and more connected to this life inside me. He or she was part of me. Part of Jaxon—the man I loved. Because despite what happened, and all the craziness I was still trying to wrap my head around, I hadn't stopped loving him. I wasn't sure that was even possible.

Fated mates…

Jaxon's words echoed in my head. He'd said it so many times, and to some degree I was beginning to understand what he might have meant. I felt a bond to him like I'd never felt with anyone. Something that defied explanation, much like the bond I'd had with my twin. But different. Being together just felt right. Like it was meant to be. Fate, I supposed.

I swallowed, not sure what to say to Liam. I couldn't promise him anything because I didn't know what Jaxon was thinking, but I knew I wanted the four of us to be a family just like Liam did.

"You have to take him back," he repeated. "The baby deserves to have his father in his life. I never—" His voice hitched. "I never had that."

He was right, but hearing him say that was devastating. He was so astute for an eight-year-old.

I had the opportunity to make things right. To give Liam the family unit he'd never had but always wanted. I couldn't lose him. I wouldn't.

But that was easier said than done. At the end of the day, our fate would be decided by a judge. All I could do was fight my hardest and hope the judge did the right thing.

"Everything is going to be okay," I promised Liam, hoping with everything I had that I wasn't telling him a lie.

My stomach fluttered again, and I wondered if the baby could sense my unease. I pressed my palms to my belly, thinking about the child I was carrying. A shifter.

Maybe everything *would* be okay. Maybe all I needed was time to get used to the idea of shifters. Despite the horror I'd felt when Jaxon had revealed his true nature to me, I knew it didn't change who he really was. A warm, kind, loving man who loved me as much as I loved him. So what if he was a wolf shifter? My baby was too. Our baby.

Maybe being with a shifter wasn't nearly as bad as I'd built it up to be. How could it, when I loved this baby completely?

I vowed then and there that after the hearing, I'd talk to Jaxon. See if we could work through this.

But first… First I had to get through the hearing and hopefully come out on the other side with Liam by my side.

***

I sat at the table at the front of the courtroom, wringing my hands together. Judge Roberts seemed nice enough, though he was stern.

Okay, here we go.

Mrs. Pinder had just been called to the stand to testify. I reached over and squeezed Liam's hand in reassurance. I could only hope she was still on my side like she'd seemed to be the last few times we'd talked. Of course, Jaxon had been there then. He seemed to charm her.

I glanced around the courtroom for the dozenth time, hoping against hope I'd see Jaxon. Did he remember today was the hearing? I couldn't imagine he would forget. Why wasn't he here then? Had my argument with Jaxon really done that much damage that he'd forsake Liam? I had to hope not. Fighting to push those thoughts aside, I focused on Mrs. Pinder and the judge.

"I've spent months following Mr. Baldwin's case, Your Honor," she said, sitting up tall with her hands folded primly in her lap. Her face was just as stern as the judge's. "I have to say, I've had plenty of concerns throughout that time. Mr. Baldwin's physical disability keeps him from continuing in his chosen field of employment, which of course has contributed to his financial hardship."

Frustration bubbled up in my chest, but I tried to keep my face blank. I couldn't let Liam see how this turn of events was upsetting me. I'd started to believe she was on our side, that she would recommend the adoption, but here she was listing out all the reasons why I might not be able to care for Liam. My heart pounded as she continued.

"Mr. Baldwin's situation is dire, and I worry he won't be able to provide for Liam the way the boy needs."

She continued on for a few minutes, saying much of the same, but never really coming to a definite conclusion. She didn't say outright she would advise against the adoption, but she didn't paint a great picture, either.

Despite my resolve to make sure I walked out of here with Liam as my official son, I started to panic. My pulse pounded, racing through my veins, the rush of blood filling my ears.

Breathe. Just breathe.

My attention was drawn back to the judge when he spoke directly to me. "Mr. Baldwin, I'd like to meet with Liam privately in my chambers."

I nodded, swallowing against the tightness in my throat. "Yes, of course," I practically croaked.

Liam looked at me, worry marring his features, and I squeezed his hand again. "It will be okay. Just answer the judge's questions honestly. He'll see the truth of the matter."

I wasn't so sure after Mrs. Pinder's testimony, but I had to hold on to any shred of hope I could. Mrs. Pinder hadn't mentioned Jaxon at all. Like she wasn't even taking him into account as far as my ability to raise Liam went. It frustrated me to no end, especially after she'd told Jaxon our relationship practically guaranteed her stamp of approval.

Liam stood and followed the judge out of the courtroom, and I was left to sit and worry. A few minutes later, I heard the doors at the entrance of the courtroom swing open. I was too lost in my thoughts for it to properly register, until I felt a tingling along my spine, a visceral awareness that penetrated right down to the bone. I shifted in my seat and glanced behind me, and nearly fell off my chair.

Jaxon stood there, just inside the mahogany double doors, his gaze fixed on me. He was here! Despite everything that happened, he was here to offer his support. His green eyes blazed with fiery determination, and my pulse skipped a beat in response.

How could I have doubted he'd be here? I knew he wouldn't let Liam down. And Jaxon wasn't alone. Behind him stood the man he'd introduced as his father—Greer. I recognized Linc, and some of the other men I'd seen in Greer's office. All standing together, a wall of unity. They were all here for Liam—and by association, me.

That knowledge rocketed through me, and I didn't know what to make of it.

Before I could get up or Jaxon could come my way, the judge reappeared from his chambers, Liam following behind. His eyes lit up when he saw Jaxon and his…family? Pack mates? I didn't really know how all that worked, but I was certain they were all shifters.

Liam rejoined me and took his seat, and we watched together as Jaxon and the rest filed into seats a few rows back from where we were sitting. I turned back around as the judge took his seat at his bench, but I still felt Jaxon's gaze on me.

"He's here, Uncle Bryce," Liam whispered, a smile on his face. "Everything's going to be okay now."

I hoped so too, but I didn't have the complete assurance Liam did. There was so much at play here. I was just about to ask him how the conversation with the judge had gone, but then Judge Roberts was speaking again, calling the courtroom to order.

"Is there anyone else who would like to speak on Mr. Baldwin's behalf for the adoption of Liam Baldwin?"

"Yes, Your Honor," a voice said from behind me.

I whipped around to find Linc standing up, giving the judge a solemn nod. My heart pounded furiously. What was Linc going to say?

Linc took the stand.

"Please state your name and tell the court how you know Mr. Baldwin," the judge said.

Linc nodded. "My name is Linc Travers. My son plays baseball with Liam. I've had the privilege of being their coach, alongside my friend Jaxon Parsons. Over the past few months, I've been witness to Bryce's interactions with Liam. I have to say, I've never seen a man who would go to such lengths to care for a child. He's had his share of obstacles for sure, but it's obvious he would do anything for Liam, and that nothing will stop Bryce from giving Liam the very best life he possibly can. Liam lacks for nothing from Bryce. He may struggle financially and physically, but he makes sure Liam has everything he needs. His love, most of all, which I think counts for more than anything."

He went on to provide a few examples at the judge's request, and my heart was full of gratitude. Linc believed everything he was saying, that much was clear. Even if Jaxon had put Linc up to this, every word was utterly sincere.

When he finished with his statement, Jaxon's father stood next, saying he'd like to speak as well. I almost couldn't believe it. When Lorelei was still alive it had been just the three of us, standing together against the world. After her death, Liam and I tried to remain positive, but there were times we felt alone. To feel this kind of unwavering support not only took me by surprise, it gave me hope.

Jaxon had said the pack was like family. That they all took care of each other. I was seeing that now. It made me see the pack in a whole new light.

Greer took the stand and introduced himself, then dove right in, his eyes full of compassion as he spoke. "As a single father, I know how hard it can be to bring up a child on your own."

I glanced back at Jaxon. His gaze locked with mine, and his lips curved in a small smile. I offered a tiny smile in return, then directed my attention back to Greer.

"It takes a community to raise a child, no matter if you're a single parent or not, and I'm here to tell you Bryce has the backing of all my family and friends. Anything he might ever need, all he has to do is ask and we'd be there in an instant."

I thought again of how tightly knit this group of shifters must be. What would it be like to be a part of that? To know it wouldn't just be Jaxon helping me raise Liam and the baby—if he was willing to move past my hurtful words—but the entire pack as well.

Suddenly, all my fears about shifters seemed entirely unfounded. These were good people—the best I'd ever known. I could see where Jaxon got his desire to protect and take care of others from. His dad was a shining example of love and encouragement. There was a subtle fierceness to him that proved he would go to any length for those he loved. Something else he shared with Jaxon.

Greer finished his speech, and I felt more optimistic than I had in days.

Judge Roberts thanked him and scanned the room. "Is there anyone else who would like to speak on Mr. Baldwin's behalf?"

I could feel the air shift as someone immediately stood a few rows back. I knew without looking that it was Jaxon. I heard his footsteps on the polished wood floor, and I risked a peek at him as he passed by me, heading to the stand.

I felt a flurry of emotions inside me. Love and hope. But also a touch of anxiety. Whatever he had to say could very well sway the judge one way or the other. I closed my eyes and breathed deeply, drawing up every bit of strength I had in me to not fall apart right there.

Mine and Liam's entire future hinged on this moment. It was in Jaxon's hands now.

I just prayed it would be enough.

Chapter 19 - Jaxon

I took the stand, my eyes never leaving Bryce's. There was such a flood of emotion pouring from him, and despite everything he'd said the other night, I knew we would overcome this. We would work through any lingering issues, and then we would be a family.

I could see the love shining within him. My wolf rumbled, eager to claim our mate. To make him mine for good. We would get there. First, I had an obstacle to vanquish—making sure when we left this courtroom it was with Liam by our sides.

"Please state your name and relationship to Mr. Baldwin," the judge said.

I shifted my gaze to Judge Roberts for a brief moment, sizing him up. He put on a good show, having a tough, stern exterior, but I could sense he was an omega human. I intended to use that to my advantage.

I sat up straighter, oozing confidence. I knew exactly how I felt about Bryce and what our future held. All I had to do was say the obvious.

"My name is Jaxon Parsons. Bryce is the man I love."

My gaze was back on Bryce, and the shift in him was noticeable as I publicly declared my love for him. He sat up a little straighter too, his eyes shimmering with tears. I gave him a soft smile, hoping it conveyed all the love and commitment I felt for him.

"I knew from the minute I saw Bryce he was the one for me," I said. My mind drifted back to that night three months ago at Kay's Diner. How I really had known, in ways I couldn't explain to the humans in this courtroom, that we were meant to be. "His strength and goodness were evident the minute I laid eyes on him. He wasn't—isn't—the kind of man to let anything hold him back. Despite his disabilities, he's worked hard to give Liam everything he could possibly need. Most of all, unwavering love. His devotion to Liam is one of the things that had me falling head over heels for him almost immediately."

Bryce smiled, reaching over to clasp Liam's hand. I tossed Liam a bright smile, hoping the poor kid wasn't worried sick. He grinned back, something the judge seemed to notice.

"And I didn't just fall for Bryce that day. I quickly came to love Liam too. As if he were my own."

The judge nodded, his brows knit. "That's great to hear, Mr. Parsons, but I'd like to focus on Mr. Baldwin's ability to care for Liam."

I cut my eyes to Bryce and gave him an easy smile. "Of course. It was immediately obvious that Bryce was willing to do anything for Liam, to make any sacrifice necessary. And I've only seen more evidence of that in the months that followed. No matter what, Bryce has done everything in his power to provide for Liam. He's given him a warm, loving home, settled him in a community where he's thriving. Yes, there were times that his physical pain was a struggle, but his inner strength more than makes up for it. In fact, I can honestly say I've never witnessed so strong a love between a father and son."

And I knew Bryce would be like that with our own child. He would be an amazing father, and I couldn't wait to raise our pup with him and Liam.

"Yes, Liam is technically his nephew, but I know better than anyone that you can love a child as your own even if you aren't their biological father." I looked at my own father then, and saw him nodding in encouragement, his face full of pride. "The love Bryce has for Liam has shown me what an amazing man and father he is."

I looked at Bryce, then back at Judge Roberts. "And I know he will be the best father to our unborn child."

His eyebrows rose. He didn't know that part. "That's right. We're going to be a family soon. Raising our child along with Liam. We'll be able to give them both everything they need. In fact, Bryce's finances or disability shouldn't even be a factor now. I intend to give them the very best life has to offer."

Judge Roberts cleared his throat. "That's all well and good, Mr. Parsons, but unfortunately, your status is not Mr. Baldwin's status. Your financial situation cannot be taken into account when evaluating Mr. Baldwin's ability to provide for young Liam."

I caught Bryce's eyes again, seeing the worry that flitted over his face. His eyes were glistening with unshed tears, and he worried his bottom lip with his teeth. The judge didn't think that was enough? Fine, I'd go a step further.

I hoped Bryce didn't react badly to what I said next, but I meant every damn word of it.

"I understand that, Your Honor. But you should know that Bryce is my fiancé. We'll be married as soon as possible—just after the baby is born." Marriage was sort of the human equivalent of claiming a mate—only our bonds as fated mates surpassed any marriage vows. We would be connected in every way, mated for life. I couldn't say that in front of a courtroom of humans, but I thought I made my point.

"I want to wait until he gives birth so there isn't any unnecessary burden on Bryce during this time. He's dealing with enough as it is—handling it excellently, but still. This adoption has been stressful. Bryce needs the assurance we can finally be a family. If the adoption isn't approved, it will put Bryce under so much pressure it would be detrimental to our baby. I refuse to allow that to happen."

Maybe I was going a bit far with my insistence, but fuck it. I leveled Judge Roberts with a firm look, bordering on a glare, letting him know in no uncertain terms I wasn't going to put Bryce or the baby at risk. My alpha dominance was coming out, even more potent now I was pack leader, but I shouldn't have to use it. This adoption shouldn't even be up for debate. Bryce was an amazing father, and he deserved to adopt Liam more than anyone. And it was also the right thing for Liam.

"I protect what's mine, Your Honor," I added. "And Liam and Bryce are mine. I love them both with all my heart and know we have a wonderful future ahead of us as a family." I paused for effect. "So can I finally take my family home where they belong so we can get on with our lives together?"

The judge let out a little chuckle. "Thank you for your spirited testimony, Mr. Parsons. You've given me plenty to think about."

I nodded, standing and making my way off the stand. I'd done everything I could at this point.

As I passed Bryce, my wolf clawed at my consciousness, demanding I take my mate in my arms. However, I knew I had to respect the court, so I forced myself to keep moving, but I couldn't take my eyes off him.

His eyes were wide, full of longing as he stared back. The link between us was strung tight, and I could feel the love coming off him in waves. I couldn't resist reaching out to touch his shoulder, though. I paused, looking down and smiling at him tenderly.

"I love you so much," I said, barely a whisper. His eyes sparkled, and his throat bobbed as he swallowed, overcome with emotion.

I squeezed his shoulder, then gave Liam a little wink and made my way back to my seat. I wanted nothing more than to sit with them while the judge made his decision, but I took comfort in sitting with my pack.

"There's a lot to consider here," Judge Roberts said. "Thank you, everyone, for your testimonies. Normally, I'd return to my chambers to deliberate, but I don't think that's necessary in this case."

I gripped my thighs. The moment of truth.

"Mr. Baldwin." Bryce straightened his already stiff shoulders, his attention on the judge. "In light of everything that's been said today, the court sees it to be in Liam's best interest to remain with you. You're granted full custody with the adoption awarded, effective immediately. Congratulations!"

He emphasized it with a bang of his gavel, and the courtroom erupted in cheers. Even Mrs. Pinder was smiling.

I was on my feet in less than a second, barely noticing my father's slap on the back and my pack's congratulatory exclamations. I strode right down the aisle and to the table.

Liam and Bryce were on their feet already, clinging to each other. Liam was laughing through his tears of joy, and Bryce stared down at him with all his love.

The next minute, they were both in my arms.

"Jaxon," Bryce said, his voice choked with tears. He looked up at me in wonder. "You did it."

"You did it, Bryce. This was preordained. Liam belongs with you." I gripped him around the waist, pulling him tighter, and Liam put his arms around both of us, beaming.

"No," Bryce said softly. "We did it. Together."

A wave of relief washed over me. I'd known, deep down, this would all work out, that I would have my mate, my family, but to hear him say that gave me the assurance I needed.

I reached up and brushed his hair back from his forehead. "I love you, Bryce. With everything in me. Can you ever forgive me for not telling you sooner?"

His brow furrowed, and he shook his head. "You know, I should be the one asking you that. I said terrible things to you."

"None of that matters now. All that matters is that we're together. That we can finally be the family we were meant to be. If that's what you want."

A smile flitted across his face. "Do you even have to ask?"

I grinned, looking down at Liam then back at Bryce. "In that case, come home with me. I don't want to wait another minute to start our life together."

Bryce's eyes welled with tears, this time a few of them spilling over. "Yes. Absolutely yes."

"Yeah!" Liam cheered, breaking our hug so he could pump the air with his fist.

I laughed and ruffled his hair. "Good. Because I've already arranged to have your stuff packed up and moved out to my place."

Bryce huffed out a short chuckle. "Pretty sure of yourself there, aren't you?"

I grinned, leaning in to give him a chaste kiss—we were still in the courtroom, after all. "I just know what I want. And I wouldn't have it any other way."

"Hmm," he murmured. "I'm starting to see how deep this shifter alpha thing goes." Then he grinned mischievously.

"Oh, you have no idea," I said, a low growl rumbling in my chest. "I'm going to take care of you in ways you never imagined." Then remembering little ears were listening, I cleared by throat. "You and the baby. I'm going to pamper you both throughout the rest of your pregnancy." I gave him a wink.

He laughed again. "I think we need to get started on this immediately."

I cupped his face, staring into his eyes. In that moment I didn't give a shit where we were or who saw us. I needed to feel my mate. I lowered my lips to his and kissed him. Softly, slowly.

We were walking out of this place together today. As a family. My mate. My son. And my little pup growing in Bryce's belly. From here on out, I knew we would be able to handle anything that came our way. Because we were a unit now, a true family.

I couldn't wait to make him and Liam mine in every way, marking them with a claiming bite. The two of them joining the pack.

But for now, I was content to hold them in my arms and know nothing else mattered because we had each other.

Chapter 20 - Bryce

"Time to wake up, sleepy head," a voice murmured in my ear.

I blinked, a smile growing on my lips as I woke up to Jaxon's kisses on my neck. He had his arm slung around me from behind, and his hand splayed out across my growing belly.

I wiggled back against him, feeling his bare cock hard against my ass. "Mmm, can we stay in bed a little bit longer?"

Jaxon chuckled, dark and full of promise. "Don't tempt me."

I smiled contentedly and snuggled in closer, resting my hand on top of his. The last two months had been about as perfect as I could have imagined. Right after we left the courtroom the day I was awarded custody, Jaxon took us straight out to his place, not willing to wait another moment to start our life together.

He'd been just as attentive as he promised, in every way. I bit my lip, thinking of the way he'd made love to me last night, taking his time to explore me thoroughly, and there was plenty to explore of me these days.

At over four months pregnant, there was no hiding it anymore. Not that I wanted to. I displayed my baby bump proudly, thrilled that Jaxon's child was growing inside me.

He rubbed his thumb in slow circles over my bare stomach. "Any guesses what the baby will be?"

I laughed and rolled to my back so I could look up at him. "Well, a shifter. We know that much."

There was no denying that. Every day that passed with shifter DNA mingling in my blood, I felt stronger. More powerful. Interestingly, even more connected to Jaxon in a way I didn't quite know how to explain. I was virtually pain-free, not needing my cane at all anymore. Every once in a while, my limp made a reappearance, but other than that I felt better than I had in a long time.

"Obviously," Jaxon replied with a cocky grin, causing me to roll my eyes, though I secretly loved how his alpha tendencies often came out in all their glory. He arched a brow. "Boy or girl?"

I shrugged. We'd had this conversation hundreds of times already. I'd wanted to wait and be surprised. Jaxon couldn't find out soon enough, ready to go out and buy *everything* for the baby. We settled on a compromise.

We would have Dr. Reed determine the gender of the baby, then seal the results away in an envelope to be discovered later at a gender reveal party. Jaxon had pulled out all the stops, making it a huge event with the whole pack. It was sweet, really. That softer side of Jaxon only I got to see.

"I guess we'll know soon enough," I said, glancing at the clock. Jaxon had been right. It was way past time to get up if we wanted to make it to the doctor's appointment on time.

I hopped out of bed. "I need to get a shower."

Jaxon followed behind me. "Need any help?"

"Not unless you want to explain to Dr. Reed why we're late," I said, laughing.

For a minute, he looked tempted to do just that, but then he grabbed my hand and yanked me to him, crushing his mouth to mine in a searing kiss. I moaned, my body immediately responding to his touch.

He broke away from me, though, a wicked gleam in his eyes. "Later," he promised.

I groaned. Now he had me all worked up. Guess it would have to be a cold shower…

An hour later, we were at Timberwood Cove General, tucked away in a dark room where Dr. Reed was getting ready to perform the sonogram. I lay on the bed, my stomach exposed. Jaxon stood by my side, his fingers twined with mine.

"Okay, dads. You ready?" Dr. Reed asked.

Jaxon had informed me that Dr. Reed wasn't just the family doctor, but the pack doctor. It made more sense now why he'd insisted we go to her, and Dr. Reed had been wonderful with me.

She talked to us now as she covered my stomach in gel and began moving the sonogram wand around.

"So right now, I'm just going to get some measurements, make sure the pup is growing well and that we're on track for the anticipated delivery date." She took pictures, and I stared in wonder at the images on the screen.

"Our baby," I said in awe, squeezing Jaxon's hand.

He squeezed back, then leaned closer to the screen. "What's that?" he asked, pointing.

"That's an arm," Dr. Reed replied, and I cocked my head, trying to orient myself to what I was seeing.

It was amazing. She pointed out the different body parts. "Ten fingers and ten toes. A strong, steady heart." She turned to us and smiled. "This one's going to be a strong one."

"Boy or girl?" Jaxon asked.

I swatted him on the arm. "You'll find out soon enough. Give me this little bit of suspense."

He sighed, like I was asking him for more than he could bear, but then he winked at me, showing me he was joking.

"Will you be at the party tonight, Dr. Reed?" I asked.

"Absolutely. I wouldn't miss this."

Jaxon smiled proudly. "I guess you'll put the results in an envelope for us to take home?"

I laughed. "No, no. I've already arranged for Dr. Reed to hand it off to Linc personally. No peeking for you."

He groaned. "Fine…"

Dr. Reed gave us some advice on what to expect for the next month. The baby would continue to move more and get stronger. Wow. It was already so active, like it couldn't wait to get out here in the world. I couldn't imagine what *more* active would be like.

We thanked her and headed to the car, Jaxon's arm around my waist. He helped me into the car, then we were back on the road to Jaxon's house. *Our house.* I smiled. It was ours now. Our home. Our life. Our family.

I couldn't wait to get back to the house. I'd been waiting for this appointment, to make sure we got a good report, to talk to Jaxon about something that had been on my mind more and more lately.

What he'd said before, about a claiming bite. About making me his forever. Claiming me as his true mate. I didn't fully understand it, but from what I gathered from the little things he'd said here and there over the months, there was even more to it than I realized.

Plus, Liam had been talking about wanting to become a wolf, even though I hadn't told him what Jaxon said. He was obviously hearing things from Cole. Jaxon had also mentioned how it would heal me completely. It was all very confusing, but I was ready to ask him about it. Ready to take the next step with him.

"You're quiet over there," Jaxon said after we'd been on the road a while. "What are you thinking about?"

I turned to him, biting my lip.

His brow furrowed. "Everything okay?"

I nodded. "More than okay. Jaxon, I've been thinking. I want to make our relationship as official as we can. I want you to claim me. As soon as the baby's born. I'm ready."

The look of surprise on his face was almost instantly replaced with joy. His eyes lit up, a smile spread his lips wide, and he turned to me excitedly. "Bryce, there's nothing I'd love more than to claim you."

"So what does that entail, exactly?"

"You know about fated mates," he said. "Well, when I claim you, a bond will form between us. A connection that can't be broken. But not just with us, with our wolves."

Our wolves.

"You'll become a shifter, Bryce. You'll have a wolf inside you."

That was one part that baffled me. I guessed I wouldn't fully understand until I'd experienced it. One thing I did understand was that I wasn't afraid, not if it meant Jaxon and I would be mated for life.

"And our wolves... I don't know exactly because I've never felt it, but apparently our wolves will bond as well." Jaxon pulled the car to a stop when we arrived home, then turned to face me.

"Just to let you know, we don't have to wait until the baby is born. It won't hurt you or the baby for me to give you a claiming bite." His eyes darkened slightly. "You wouldn't believe how hard it's been not to claim you already." He reached out and ran a hand over my neck. "I could claim you right now. You just wouldn't be able to have your first shift until after the baby is born."

"What about Liam?" I asked.

Jaxon nodded, his thumb stroking my neck now. "Of course. I'll claim him as my own. He'll become a shifter too."

I grinned. "You really will be his hero then."

I wanted this. I knew I did, but I'd always thought that when I got married, I'd have a wedding. "I know you said shifters don't get married, but...could we have a ceremony or something?" I shrugged and bit my lip. What if he thought that was silly? "I mean, I don't know how this really works."

He nodded, a smile curving his lips. "If that's what you want, that's what you'll have. It's not always what shifters choose to do now, but traditionally there would be a claiming ceremony."

His hand tightened slightly on my throat, and his voice was husky when he said, "Are you sure you don't want me to claim you now. Ceremony later?" There was a glint in his eyes, something primal, which I was starting to recognize as his wolf near the surface, and just like that, I wanted him.

I strained toward him, still in my seatbelt. "Let's go inside."

Jaxon's green eyes shone. "Liam's at the lodge helping out with the party until tonight, isn't he?"

I nodded, fumbling with my seatbelt. We couldn't get out of the car fast enough. Practically racing into the house, Jaxon pulled me along, opened the door, then yanked me inside. It continually amazed me how I hardly felt the pain of my old injuries.

With a feral growl, he kicked the door shut and pushed me back against it. His breath was hot on my throat as he traced his teeth along the vein. I moaned, suddenly aching for him to bite me, needing to be as close to him as possible.

Jaxon gripped my wrists and pulled them above my head, grinding his hips against my throbbing cock. "Are you sure you don't want me to claim you now?"

"Impatient much?" I let my head fall back against the door as he nipped lightly at my neck. Electricity shot through me, and when I opened my eyes I could see the elemental instinct in his piercing gaze as he lifted his head. I licked my lips, wanting it as much as he did, but I still had enough wits about me to know I wanted to do this right.

I shook my head. "Ceremony..." I managed to say, distracted by the feel of his cock pressing into my hip.

He drew in a ragged breath, then nodded. "Okay," he said, his voice low and strained. "But I can't promise to be gentle with you right now."

A thrill raced through me, igniting my blood. "Who said I wanted you to?"

It was like I'd unleashed the beast. A growl erupted from Jaxon's throat and he reached over his head to pull his shirt off. He didn't even bother taking mine off. He just dug his fist into the fabric and pulled—hard enough to rip it from my body. I gasped, incredibly turned on by this side of him.

He scraped his fingers down my chest, then leaned in and caught my nipple between his teeth, tugging hard. The sharp bite had my cock jerking in response. My body ached, my ass begging to be filled.

"Jaxon, please..."

When he didn't act fast enough, I gripped his dick through his jeans. A wild glint flashed in his eyes and a wicked smirk appeared on his face.

"So that's how you want to do this? You think you're in charge?"

I squeezed him, and his cock pulsed in the palm of my hand. "I think I am right now."

The alpha in him roared to life, and he picked me up. "You're going to pay for that."

I grinned. I loved Jaxon like this. I loved all the ways he was gentle with me too, but sometimes, like now, it felt good to really let loose. I idly wondered if sex with him would be even more intense once he'd claimed me.

When he put me down in the bedroom, I instantly backed him up against the wall. Jaxon's eyes flashed dangerously but he let me take my time exploring his body. I traced my fingers over his broad shoulders, squeezing his biceps, teasing up his abs. When I got to the waistband of his jeans I started to undo the buttons, cursing softly when my fingers wouldn't obey me. Jaxon chuckled, and then helped me, stripping out of his jeans and then quickly ridding me of mine.

Both naked, I took over where I left of, reaching for Jaxon's cock and gripping it firmly in my fist. He grunted and thrust into me. I'd only stroked him a couple times when he took over again, grabbing my hips and spinning me around until his chest was against my back. He pinned me to him, one hand over my chest, the other on my hip. Then he ground his cock against me.

I moaned, my body aching for more. My slick pooled, coating Jaxon's cock as he slid it up and down against my hole. He scraped his teeth along my neck again, and I thought I might die if he didn't fuck me right now. He could go ahead and claim me and I wouldn't complain, but he kept his word, grabbing my chin instead so he could angle my head back and take my mouth.

More, more, more...

It was all I could think as he devoured me whole, all his pent-up passion bursting forth. I reveled in it, soaking in every sensation that assaulted my body. I didn't even have to beg this time. He wanted the same thing. More.

Jaxon plunged into me in one swift thrust of his hips, burying his cock balls deep inside my ass. I cried out, my body practically vibrating. He fucked me hard from behind, his desperation to have me driving him on. I felt the same desperate need build inside me. My body was on fire, my skin stinging as he raked his fingers over me.

Jaxon held us together, his grip on me unyielding when he clutched me even tighter to his chest. I dropped my head back on his shoulder, moaning as he drove into me over and over. Just as my balls tightened and the base of my spine started to tingle, I felt his knot form, swelling up inside me, so thick and so, so good.

I gasped as I came violently, shuddering as wave after wave of intense pleasure ripped through my body. Jaxon growled in my ear, escalating to nearly a roar as he came deep inside me.

My body felt like jelly, so Jaxon continued to hold me until his knot receded, and then he caught me up in his arms and carried me to our bed, sprinkling me with kisses. He cuddled up behind me, and we lay there catching our breath.

That had been...incredible. I wanted him to claim me now more than ever. I had a feeling I wouldn't be able to resist his charm for long and I'd give in to him, much like I had with the gender reveal.

We might just have to push that claiming ceremony up a bit.

***

Later that night it seemed like the whole pack was gathered in the lodge. As we made our way through the front doors, it looked like we were the last ones to arrive.

That would be my fault.

I'd kept Jaxon in bed all afternoon. It was either that or tie him down to keep him from running over and choking the gender out of Linc before the party. I hadn't minded one bit.

Greetings filled the air as we made our way through the crowd. I saw many faces I recognized, but not all. The whole pack really had come out to support their alpha. It was incredible watching Jaxon lead his pack the past couple months. He was a natural leader. Commanding and charismatic, but also understanding and loyal to his last bone.

"Okay, let's do this thing!" Jaxon called out, pulling me along behind him to the front of the room. The entire lodge had been turned into a wonderland, lights and flowers and baby stuff everywhere.

Linc, Greer, Liam and Cole had put all this together, but no doubt Jaxon had given his input. If this is what they did for a simple gender reveal party I couldn't begin to imagine what a claiming ceremony might be like. A shiver of anticipation ran through me—for that, and to find out if we were having a boy or a girl.

Jaxon apparently wanted to get the party started by doing the reveal right away.

"Thanks so much, everyone, for coming out this evening. I'm so happy to have you all be part of this momentous revelation." Apparently he had a flair for the dramatic too.

I grinned up at him. "Okay, you ready then?" I looked into the crowd. "Linc?"

He was at the front of the group, watching and smiling. "All good to go."

"Awesome," Jaxon said, then gave me a quick kiss before reaching for a string above our heads. We were standing right under a bag of balloons that would rain down on us in blue or pink. "Ready, baby?"

I reached up and wrapped my hand around his, then we pulled together. Hundreds of pink balloons cascaded around the room, confetti added for good measure.

Jaxon turned me in his arms, beaming at me. "A girl! We're having a girl!"

I flung my arms around him, so excited. What had I been thinking wanting to wait until she was born? Now I could spend the next few months really preparing a palace for our new princess. Jaxon was going to spoil this baby girl rotten, I just knew it.

He pulled back, looking at me in wonder. Then the next thing I knew, he was stepping back. Going down on one knee. Taking my hand. I gasped, my other hand flying to my mouth. Jaxon stared up at me, his eyes shining with adoration.

"Bryce Baldwin," he said. "I love you. You are my fated mate, the other half of my soul. And I want to make you mine in every way."

I should have blushed, standing in front of everyone like this, but I only had eyes for him as he looked up at me earnestly.

"Will you be mine forever? Will you let me claim you and make you mine?"

My smile stretched my cheeks wide. "You know I will," I answered, and I nearly sank to my knees right there to kiss him, but the fact we had an audience came sharply back into focus when I heard Liam and Cole giggling. Jaxon cocked his head, giving me a wry grin.

"Liam, come here," he said, stretching his hand out.

Liam's eyes went wide before he slowly walked toward Jaxon and me. I had a pretty good idea what Jaxon was up to when he took Liam's hand in his.

"And Liam. I love you, son. I want to claim you as well, as my son and as a wolf."

Liam's smile lit the room, even as tears overflowed and fell down his cheeks. He swallowed hard and looked at Jaxon. "I would love that."

It felt like my heart my burst at that moment. Jaxon gave him a wink, then stood up, pulling me into his arms. He began to pull me in for a kiss, but Liam's voice rang out, startling us apart.

"This means I'm gonna be a wolf," he shouted, as if it were all just now clicking into place. He let out a whoop then ran back to Cole in the crowd.

That seemed to be the signal to get the party started because conversation filled the room once more, and someone turned on music that pounded through the speakers. I laughed. So it was going to be that kind of party, then. The Timberwood Cove wolves apparently liked to party.

Jaxon took that moment to pull me back in his arms. We swayed softly to the music, and I didn't even care we were slow dancing to an upbeat song while people began bopping around us. I was in a little bubble right now, just the two of us.

"I love you," he murmured, resting his forehead against mine and placing his hands on my hips.

"And I love you," I replied, bringing his lips to mine in a tender kiss. I didn't know how long we stayed like that, swaying there locked in each other's arms.

Eventually I became aware of the scent of steak wafting through the air. My stomach growled.

Jaxon pulled back and laughed. "Time to feed the baby?"

"What can I say, the baby likes steak."

We made our way around the room, stopping and talking to people along the way. The party was in full swing, music blasting, dancers in the middle of the floor. All the doors were open to the wraparound porch.

"That way," I said, pointing toward the back of the lodge where the delicious aromas were coming from.

"Let's go," Jaxon said, pulling me along.

We spent the next several hours celebrating. The entire pack thrilled their leader would be a father. And of a baby girl.

I shook my head as I walked out to the deck a bit later. Jaxon was busy talking shop inside, and I wanted a little fresh air. Luckily it was a bit less crowded back here now the barbeque was over. I stepped up to the deck railing and leaned on it, scanning the trees and rolling hills in the distance. This was my new home. My life had changed dramatically in under six months, and I wouldn't have it any other way.

Still, as I looked out at the twinkling stars I couldn't help but think about Lorelei. I wished more than anything she could be here now, a part of this, part of me. Losing my twin had taken a toll I doubt I would fully recover from. I would always miss Lori.

"You okay?" Jaxon's voice was low behind me as he stepped out onto the deck.

I turned to him, feeling my throat tighten. I nodded wordlessly, and he was by my side in a second.

"What's wrong?" He cupped my cheek and studied my eyes.

I swallowed against the threat of tears. "I was just thinking about my sister. How I wish she could be here to witness all of this."

Jaxon pulled me to him, resting my head on his shoulder. "Oh, baby. I know. I wish I could give you that."

I pulled back, looking up at him. "You might not be able to do that, but you can give me one thing."

"Anything. You know that."

"Now we know the baby is a girl, I want to name her after my sister. In fact, there's no other name I'd even consider. The baby's name will be Lori, and that's final."

Jaxon chuckled at how zealous I'd become over it. "There's no way I'd deny you that. I can't think of any better name for our daughter than Lori."

My heart swelled. Jaxon would never deny me anything, and of course he couldn't think of a better name. I smiled. "It's official then. We'll name her Lori Lee."

"Perfect."

I echoed his sentiment because there was no better word to describe our life than that: Perfect.

Chapter 21 - Jaxon

The summer breeze ruffled my hair, the tail of my tuxedo flapping behind me. I'd pulled it off. The claiming ceremony of the century. It would go down in Timberwood Cove Wolf Pack history, that was for sure.

Amazing, considering I'd only had a few weeks to pull it off, but Bryce wanted this traditional ceremony, and I'd pulled out all the stops to make it happen before we both gave in to the desire for me to claim him.

I stood at the head of the aisle we'd set up behind the lodge, scanning the multitude that had gathered. Everyone from the pack had turned out for their lead alpha's claiming ceremony.

I couldn't have pulled this off without help, though. Linc had been an amazing best man. My dad had been right there, with Liam and Cole. Some of the others had pitched in too, doing all we could to give Bryce the dream wedding he'd always wanted.

A golden hue washed over everything. We'd timed the ceremony just before sunset when the late summer sun cast everything in a magical glow. The golden hour. I couldn't think of a better place for us to exchange our vows and commit our lives to each other.

White chairs, filled to capacity, spanned the length of the grassy clearing just before the tree line. Flowers were everywhere, bright whites and yellows and blues. The arch I was standing in front of was covered in vines and roses, their sweet, heady scent filling the air. I breathed it in deeply, then blew out heavily. Linc chuckled from where he stood beside me.

"Nervous?"

"Not at all," I replied with a grin. "I'm just ready to get this show on the road."

"Sounds about right." He rested a hand on my shoulder. "Jaxon, I'm so happy for you. And proud of you."

My throat tightened and I nodded. "Thank you. It means the world to me to have you stand by my side today."

To Linc's left stood my father. They were both decked out in fine suits. We'd made this quite the formal affair. A traditional claiming ceremony would normally be out on the same rock where I'd become lead alpha, but there wasn't enough room there for the scope of the ceremony I'd wanted to give Bryce. What we'd come up with was formal, to be sure, but it also had a modern, human twist. It was the perfect blend of shifter and human traditions. Perfect for me and Bryce.

"I mean it. The things you've done for Bryce and Liam are some of the most alpha things I've ever witnessed anyone do. I'm proud to stand beside you as your best friend. And even prouder to call you my alpha."

I thought I might get choked up from his words, but when my father stepped forward and clasped my shoulder, it made it infinitely more emotional.

"He's right, son. You're the best leader this pack has ever known. I'm so proud of you," he said.

I'd delved right into my duties as pack alpha, setting up shop in my father's office while he enjoyed the perks of retirement. Though I really hadn't let him relax much as he'd had his hands full helping me with the ceremony.

The crowed murmured quietly, and birds sang in the trees behind us. Music played softly in the background. My body felt jittery. I was ready to get going with this. Ready to see my mate walk down the aisle and claim him as my own.

It was a momentous occasion. Not only was I claiming my mate—and Liam as my son—but the entire pack was gaining a lead alpha's omega. Bryce would be one of us after this. Part of the pack in every way.

Suddenly, a hush fell over the crowd as the music changed into a slower song. My heart hammered in my chest. It was time.

My father pulled me into a tight hug. "I love you, son," he said before resuming his place. Linc gave me a wink and a grin, then stepped back, clasping his hands behind his back. I assumed the same position.

Nerves jittered, and I clenched my fingers together. I stared down the aisle, where a gauzy drape acted as a veil. I could see movement behind it. Bryce. He was about to make his appearance.

The piano music resonated over the hushed silence of the gathered pack. Then it swelled, and the veil parted. All the air rushed from my lungs.

There, under a matching arch, stood my mate. My love. The man I wanted to spend the rest of my life with. To his side, clasping his hand, stood Liam. They both shone brightly enough to put the sun to shame.

My wolf howled in recognition of his mate. A warmth filled me, the connection I felt to Bryce filling the space between us more intensely than ever before. I barely restrained myself from rushing down the aisle to meet him when he took his first step.

The golden light cast a halo around the two of them as they made their way toward me. They were wearing identical white tuxedos that matched my navy one. The sun gleamed off Liam's blond hair and Bryce's sandier version. I didn't think I'd never seen anything more breathtaking. My gaze dropped to Bryce's swollen tummy. I knew he'd be even larger by the time Lori was ready to make her appearance in a few months. I couldn't wait. I found it sexy as hell to see my mate swollen with our child.

As they came closer with every step, my heart pounded. By the time he reached me, I thought I might burst. Our eyes locked, and Bryce took the final step to stand by my side with Liam taking his place just behind him.

I reached for Bryce's hand, clasping it in mine, twining my fingers with his. He squeezed back, his eyes full of adoration and anticipation. Not a hint of fear. He was as ready for this as I was, and I couldn't be more thrilled. He wanted to become a shifter, to be a part of my pack. To be my one true mate.

I swallowed against the lump in my throat. "You look breathtaking," I whispered, reaching up to brush my thumb across his cheek.

He smiled. "How did I get so lucky?"

I smiled back, hoping he knew how lucky *I* felt.

The sound of a throat clearing to my right reminded me of where I was and what I was supposed to be doing. The officiant, a shifter from our pack, smiled at me, and I nodded. It was time.

Bryce and I turned to face each other fully, and I took both of his hands in mine now, staring down into his gorgeous face. His hazel eyes with thick brows, his angular jaw, his full lips. God, I could hardly breathe.

When the officiant began speaking, I lost myself in the moment. Everything around us disappeared, leaving Bryce and I in a space where only the two of us existed. I reached out to him with my soul, finding that connection that could only exist with a fated mate. I felt his heartbeat in return, as if we were already becoming part of each other in a way I didn't really fully understand yet.

Then it was time for the vows.

I stepped closer. "Bryce Baldwin, to say I love you doesn't begin to describe the things I feel for you. You're everything to me. My joy, my happiness, my hope, my heart. You're the very air I breathe. You've seen me for who I am, and love me unconditionally, and I thank fate every day for choosing you for me. I promise to always be by your side, your partner in life. Your alpha who will care for you, love you passionately, and be the best father I can to our children. I vow to love you and spend every day showing you, for the rest of our lives. Forever and always."

Bryce's eyes were brimming with tears. Linc darted forward with the ring I'd had custom made for Bryce. It matched my lead alpha ring. Yellow gold with black etchings. Symbolizing his place beside me in the pack.

I took it and slid it on his finger, my eyes still locked with his. "I love you, Bryce."

He nodded, the tears spilling over now. I wiped them away gently with my thumb, and he drew in a tremulous breath. Then he smiled, love radiating from within.

"Jaxon Parsons, I never expected someone like you to come into my life. To turn everything I thought I knew on its head, and to give me a love I never thought I deserved. You've given me everything. A home, a family, a child, and a future I didn't even know I wanted but can now never imagine not having. I promise to love you, to stand with you and support you. To spend every day showing you just how much I love you in return. Forever and always."

My heart continued to trip-hammer. This was it. The moment I would claim him.

Except he surprised me with a token of his own. Shifters traditionally didn't wear wedding bands, so I hadn't expected this. Only it wasn't a ring.

It was a pendant, a golden wolf head with black etchings defining its features. Its eyes gleamed with twin emerald gems.

"The emeralds were my sister's," he said, then he swallowed hard, more tears threatening to spill over. "I loved her more than anything, and she would love to know something of hers is now something of yours. I always felt she was half of my soul, which I lost, but you are my true half. Wear this, close to your heart, a symbol of our souls coming together, making me whole."

My throat worked. I couldn't speak. My voice was strangled in a chokehold as a wave of emotion overcame me. Awe, gratitude, a love that didn't even have words to describe.

Bryce smiled and reached up to brush away the single tear that fell from my eye. "I love you, Jaxon."

The entire crowed was silent, witnessing this moment, so raw, so full of power. I stepped even closer, my heart nearly bursting, my wolf right there, ready to claim his mate. Bryce angled his head, exposing his neck. I could practically feel the thrum of his pulse vibrating through my body. I brought my lips to his neck, kissing him softly. He tensed slightly, and I caressed his face gently.

"Just relax," I said.

When he pushed out a breath, the tension leaving his shoulders, I bared my teeth and sank them into the vein on his neck.

All at once, I was hit with a flood of sensations. The scent of him filled my lungs, stronger than ever. I felt the beat of his heart echoing deep inside me. My wolf howled, reaching out. Now I'd made the claiming bite, his presence swept through me and into Bryce, claiming him as well.

The connection between us intensified, and it felt as if we truly were two halves of the same soul. As my wolf DNA mingled into his blood, pure and potent, I felt a spark inside him, the beginnings of his own wolf coming to life—then our wolves came together, the mate bond sealed.

When I pulled away I pressed a kiss to the wound, which had already begun to heal, and then looked into Bryce's eyes. "Are you okay?"

He smiled and reached up to brush his fingers over the closing bite mark. "The pain is already beginning to fade."

Holding him closely, I whispered, "I think it's time for me to kiss my mate."

He tilted his lips, and I settled mine over his mouth softly. A gentle brush, then another before fully capturing them. I kissed him slowly. Deeply. Tenderly and full of all the love I was feeling.

Cheers rose around us as the officiant pronounced us the mated alpha and omega of the Timberwood Cove Wolf Pack.

Joy filled my chest, and I pulled Bryce closer.

When I finally broke the kiss, I looked toward Liam. The minute my gaze fell on him, he bounced on his toes, shouting, "Bite me!"

The crowed tittered, and I smiled, going down on my knee beside Bryce and reaching out a hand to Liam.

"Liam Baldwin," I said solemnly. "I could have no greater honor than to claim you as my son. To make you part of the pack. I promise to love you and take care of you. To be your father and your leader, your friend and your support."

Liam nodded, his eyes wide, unsure what to say. I lifted his arm and rubbed the skin on the top of his forearm where I would bite him to claim him and make him a wolf.

"Are you ready for this?" I asked softly.

"Are you kidding? I've been waiting for this forever!" He grinned.

I chuckled, then brought my mouth to his arm. I bit in, hoping I didn't hurt him too much. He winced but didn't cry out. Then I felt a similar phenomenon to what happened when I claimed Bryce. My wolf reaching out, sparking a wolf to life inside of Liam, and also forging an unbreakable bond. Liam was mine. My wolf claimed him as our own.

When I pulled back, his eyes were wide again as he looked up at me. "Can I shift now?"

The crowd laughed again. "Not yet. It will be a few days before you're able to. We have to wait until my wolf's blood in flowing through your system."

I stood up, lacing my fingers with Bryce's, kissing him while resting one hand on Liam's shoulder. The pack clapped and cheered again, and the music kicked up once more.

Euphoric, I strode back up the aisle with my family. Bryce had a hand on his belly, and when he looked over at me, beaming and radiant, the only thing I thought could make my life more complete would be the birth of our baby girl.

***

I was barely hanging on. The reception had been in full swing for hours now. We'd done all the things a wedding would normally have; a first dance, cake, the works. It had been a party for the books, but all I wanted right now was to get my mate home and out of this tux. He looked so fucking sexy with his belly swollen, his hair a little messy from the dancing we'd done.

We were dancing now, a slower one, and he swayed in my arms, looking up at me with a dreamy expression. I was pretty sure I had one to match. I couldn't stop grinning.

I rested my hands on his ass and pulled him closer. "What do you say we get out of here?"

He grinned. "I think you've been patient long enough."

A growl rumbled in my chest. No kidding. I thought I'd done pretty well not dragging him home the minute the ceremony was over.

He bit his lip, his eyes darkening. "I think I'm about ready to get out of here too."

Fuck yes. That was all I needed to hear. I grabbed his hand and started pulling him toward the door. I caught Linc's eye and signaled to him. In a matter of seconds he was calling everyone up to see us off.

Liam ran forward. "Can you teach me to shift tomorrow when I come home?" He was staying at Linc's tonight.

I chuckled. "A few more days, buddy. A few more days then I promise I'll teach you, but it's not just something you learn overnight. Practice, you know how that works."

He grinned. "Well I do have the best coach ever."

Bryce smiled and pulled him into a hug. "You're absolutely right about that. You have fun with Cole tonight, okay?" He pressed a kiss to Liam's hair. "I'll see you tomorrow. Love you."

"Love you too, Dad!" He grinned up at us. "And you too, Dad."

Bryce stood still, frozen with shock at hearing Liam call him Dad. Then a huge smile spread over his face. I could sense the joy radiating from him. But then Liam went to find Cole, and the crowed pressed in around us, sending us off with congratulations.

I grinned at Bryce, then made a beeline for the door. By the time we got home my wolf was dangerously close to the surface. I slammed the car into park and then ran around to pull Bryce from it. I swept him right up in my arms and crushed my mouth to his. He moaned, slipping his hands around my neck and tugging at my hair. I scraped my teeth down to where his bite mark had faded to a light pink. He bucked in my arms, and sensations rocketed through both of us. Our wolves reaching out to each other.

With a growl, I carried him into the house and straight upstairs to the bedroom. He kissed all over my jaw, my neck, my shoulders as I carried him, like he couldn't get enough of me. God, I knew the feeling. Kicking the bedroom door open, I put him back on his feet and took his hand, then I pulled him forward, stepping over the threshold of our bedroom together. I watched his face, smiling as he took it all in.

I'd made sure this place was decked out as well. Flowers filled the room, their shadows flickering in the candlelight. The heady aroma filled my nose, mingling with Bryce's scent. Soft music played in the background. Bryce turned to me, love shining in his eyes. I knew he'd love this. I stepped toward him, but suddenly I didn't feel the irrepressible urge to just ravage him right then and there.

My wolf echoed in my mind, subdued now too at the look on our mate's face. I felt almost reverent. This moment sacred.

I wrapped my arms around him and held him closely, kissing him softly again. Wanting to savor him, to seep into his very bones. He melted against me, his kiss just as sweet. I lifted him in my arms and carried him to the bed, then slowly stripped him, taking my time, committing every second of this night to memory.

When we were both naked and spread out on the mattress, I cradled his face in my hands and stared into his eyes. "I love you, Bryce."

"I love you too."

In deference to his baby bump, I was going to suggest I take him from behind, but he must have known what I was thinking because he shook his head.

"I want you to face me. I want to see your eyes as you come inside me."

I nodded, angling his hips before carefully positioning the tip of my cock against his bud. I braced myself over him, my gaze locked on his, and our wolves whimpered with longing.

As I entered him I felt a powerful shock of heat radiate through me. I was electrified, my body feeling more alive than I thought possible. Bryce gasped, his eyes widening. He obviously felt it too.

Joined together, our wolves as one, our hearts and our spirits and our souls fully united, I was nearly overcome with emotion. I made love to him sweetly, slowly, wanting to disappear into this deluge of sensation coursing through my body and my soul.

"How do you feel?" I asked, running my lips along his mark.

"Perfect, like everything is just how it was meant to be. I love you, Jaxon."

"I love you, baby."

I brought my mouth to his, fusing us together. He was right. Everything was perfect. I had the life I'd always dreamed of. This incredible man to spend it with. And this was only the beginning.

Chapter 22 - Bryce

Four months later...

I stood in the nursery, looking at how it had all come together over the last few months. It was late, but I couldn't sleep. It was getting more and more uncomfortable now I was nine months pregnant, and I found myself in the nursery a lot at night. Earlier my back had begun to ache, and at first I wondered if it was a lingering pain from my injury, but as my wolf had formed within me, I'd been completely healed, so I knew it wasn't that.

I picked up a little stuffed wolf Linc had bought, and cradled it to my chest, knowing Lori would love it. I was sure she'd love everything to do with wolves, including her big brother, who was still learning to shift. Jaxon had been working with Liam but apparently it was harder for a human-turned-shifter than a born shifter to learn. I knew he'd get it soon. Then after Lori was born I'd no doubt need to be taught. Jaxon kept talking about going on a run together, as a family. I couldn't wait.

Running my fingers over the thick plushness of the wolf, I sighed contentedly. I had loved every minute of the last few months. Jaxon fawning over me, being together as a true family in our home, the baby growing. So many wonderful things had happened, and we still had so many more ahead of us. And I got to do it side by side with my mate. Jaxon was the best mate and alpha anyone could hope for.

A sudden pain in my back had me dropping the toy wolf and jerking up straighter with a gasp.

"You okay?"

I turned at the sound of Jaxon's voice and pressed my palm to my lower back. He was right there beside me in an instant.

"How long have you been standing there?" I asked.

"Long enough to wonder why you look like you're in pain." His eyes flashed with worry.

I shook my head. "It's nothing." Other than the backache earlier I hadn't had many issues with the pregnancy, except for sore ribs. Lori seemed to enjoy stretching out and burying her feet in them. "Probably just the baby kicking."

Jaxon moved behind me and wrapped his arms around me, covering my swollen baby bump with his hands. Nine months of pregnancy had left me *huge*.

"Let Daddy feel," he murmured.

As soon as his hands touched my stomach, I felt it again. I grunted, my body doubling over. Then I released long moan.

"Bryce?" Jaxon whipped around me, his eyes full of panic.

I panted. This wasn't a baby kicking. "I think I'm in labor."

As if to prove my words, there was a faint pop and then a flood of liquid ran down my legs.

"Oh my god." Jaxon stepped back, his legs spread wide, his fists shoved into his hair. He looked around the room like it held all the answers. "What do we do?"

I lifted an eyebrow, amused. *This* was unexpected. "I think this is the part where we go to the hospital."

"Hospital. Right." He stared at me blankly, frozen in place.

I barely held back a laugh. "Jaxon? Do I need to drive?"

A confused look crossed his face, then he shook his head, seeming to snap out if it. "No. I've got this."

He sprang into business mode. There's the alpha I knew. He pulled his phone out of his pocket and lifted it to his ear.

"You calling a cab?" I asked, teasing. The pain from that initial contraction had subsided, and I felt pretty relaxed, all things considered. I knew another would be coming soon, though. I was glad to see I had my strong support back in action so he could help me through it.

I thought I heard Linc's voice through the phone. "Jaxon? Everything okay?"

"Operation Lori has begun," he said quickly. "You know what to do."

Okay, now there was no suppressing my laughter. "Operation Lori? Really?" I shook my head and grinned at him.

He hung up the phone and shoved it back in his pocket before staring down at me, a serious look in his eyes. "I'm right here, baby. Every step of the way. You have me to count on."

He was so earnest, so sincere. My heart swelled and I fell even more in love with him. I went up on my tiptoes and pressed a quick kiss to his lips. "I know."

Just then I heard the downstairs door creak open. Even my hearing seemed to be improved as my wolf grew stronger.

"That's our cue," Jaxon said with a wink. Then he scooped me up in his arms and carried me downstairs.

Linc was standing there, keys dangling in his hand. "All ready to go? I'll take it from here."

I laughed. It was like they were on a mission. Their strategy planned out move by move. I should have expected it from Jaxon.

"Linc will stay until my father can get here to stay with Liam," Jaxon told me as he walked me out to the car. Except where the car usually sat, something was in its place. A brand-new shiny black SUV. From where the doors were open, the vehicle already running and waiting for us, I could see a pink car seat in the back.

"Jaxon? What's this?"

He grinned down at me, looking more than a little smug. "We're doing this in style, baby."

He seemed to have had thought of everything. I was eternally grateful for it too because I was starting to feel nervous. I mean, I was about to give birth to a shifter. How did someone prepare themselves for that?

But Jaxon was self-assured at my side, keeping me as relaxed as possible as he drove me to the hospital. He helped me into a wheelchair—he insisted this time—and held my hand the entire time we waited for Dr. Reed and a shifter birthing team to arrive. His attention was solely on me, making sure I was comfortable, helping me breathe through the increasingly intense contractions—this baby wanted out *now*.

He was a steady rock.

The doctors arrived and took us into a room, checked my vitals, and had me prepped for an epidural in no time, but when it was time for the cesarean, which was something both Jaxon and I had agreed on, I saw his strength waver for a second, his eyes darting from my stomach to my eyes and back again.

"Maybe you shouldn't watch," I said, smirking.

He jerked his gaze back to mine, giving me a wry grin. "We'll see."

He did end up staying by my head, holding my hand as the operation began. It was the strangest sensation, hearing everything around me but not able to see or feel anything below my waist. Jaxon's grip on my fingers tightened only a few minutes later. Dr. Reed was delivering the baby.

Jaxon stepped forward, and the look of awe and love on his face as he laid eyes on our baby had tears prickling my lids. He looked back at me, grinning, then turned back to watch. I heard a cry, and then Dr. Reed asking Jaxon if he wanted to cut the cord. Of course he said yes. And then the nurses were bundling Lori in a blanket and handing her to Jaxon.

He shook his head in amazement, his smile wide as he brought her to me. He leaned down, placing her in my arms but not letting go, and we held her together in what had to be the happiest moment of our lives.

The next few hours passed by in a cloud of baby bliss, coupled with exhaustion. Of course Lori had chosen the middle of the night to make her appearance. We got moved into a room after a little while, and Jaxon arranged for an extra hospital bed to be moved in so he could push it up against mine and sleep next to me.

He snuggled up close, determined to take care of me any way I needed. He got up through the night to change Lori, to walk around soothing her, feeding her and holding her while she slept. He'd finally fallen asleep somewhere around dawn. Now I was holding Lori in my arms, my gaze going back and forth between my daughter and my mate.

He looked strong and fierce, even in sleep, his protective streak evident from the way his arm was slung around me. I looked down at Lori, my throat tightening. It amazed me how much she looked like my twin. The downy blonde hair, her defined features. She looked just like Liam had when he was a baby. My heart swelled, feeling like I had another part of my sister here with me now. She would always be a part of me.

Jaxon stirred next to me, his eyes blinking open. A soft smile curved his lips. His jaw was extra scruffy today.

"How's my little girl this morning?" he quietly asked, pushing up on his elbow. He glanced up at me and smiled. Just as he was leaning in for a kiss, we heard a knock at the door.

"Good morning. Sorry to bother you." A nurse stood in the doorway, a friendly smile on his lips. "My name is Shawn. I'll be your daytime nurse today. I just need to check your vitals."

"Sure thing," I said, shifting Lori to Jaxon's arms. He moved off the bed and stood to the side so Shawn could do his job.

A rustle at the door caught my attention as Shawn checked my blood pressure. I turned my head to see Linc, Greer, Liam and Cole in the doorway with balloons, flowers, and bags full of gifts.

"We come baring gifts!" Linc called out, barging in and grinning. "Now let me see that baby girl!"

Shawn turned, catching sight of the four people that had just made this room a lot more crowded. His gaze roved over them, paused on Linc then snapped back to the monitor.

"Hey guys," I said, lifting my other hand in greeting. Liam rushed toward the bed, going for a hug.

"I'll be out of your way in just a moment," Shawn murmured, his gazed locked on his keyboard as he recorded his visit on my chart.

He took the blood pressure cuff off, and Liam flew into my arms. I laughed. "Careful there." I wrapped my arms around him and hugged him tightly. He squeezed me back, hard. Over his shoulder, I caught Linc staring behind us toward the door. I cut my eyes over to see what he was looking at and saw nothing but Shawn's retreating back.

I grinned, ready to tease him about crushing on my nurse when he suddenly stood and walked out of the room. Liam pulled back from my hug, demanding to see his sister, and I forgot all about whatever that was with Linc.

"Here she is," I said. Jaxon came up and leaned down, holding Lori so Liam could see.

"Meet your new sister, Lori Lee."

Liam leaned and kissed her softly on the forehead then turned to me with a grin. "She looks like Mom."

A fresh wave of tears threatened. I was so emotional right now, but what did I expect? Everyone I loved most was right here in this room with me.

"She does, Liam," Jaxon agreed.

Greer gave his congratulations, hugging Jaxon, taking his turn holding the baby. Then Liam got a turn. Cole and Linc too, when Linc finally returned.

"Okay," Liam huffed after a while, jumping up and facing Jaxon and me. "I've waited long enough. I have something to tell you."

My eyebrows flew up. What could it be? I saw Jaxon wink at him and wondered if he already knew.

"Actually, maybe I'll just show you."

He stepped back into the middle of the room, closed his eyes, then his body shimmered faintly before a pulse of heat filled the room. Then he was standing there before me, on four legs this time. I gasped and looked at Jaxon. Liam had just shifted! He stood there before us, a blond ball of fur, hazel eyes gleaming at me. He was about half the size of Jaxon's wolf.

"Liam, that was amazing!" I exclaimed as he shifted back. "When did this happen?"

He grinned. "Last night. I heard you guys leave and went back to Cole's with Linc. After Linc was asleep we snuck outside and Cole shifted. I wanted it soooo bad. And then it happened! All those things you taught me, they snapped into place."

Jaxon chuckled. "I'm glad it helped, but how about next time you don't sneak out in the middle of the night?" He gave Linc a look, and Linc looked back like he was saying, 'Really?'

I had a feeling the two of them had snuck out plenty of times when they were younger.

"I'm so proud of you, Liam," I said. He was beaming.

"I can't wait for you to shift too!"

"Soon enough," I said. "For now I'm just happy to be here with all of you."

Jaxon stroked my hair. "I couldn't have said it better. I feel like I've waited my whole life for this moment, and now it's finally here it's even more perfect than I imagined."

He kissed me softly then bent down to kiss Lori before settling down with Liam to hear all about his first shifting experience. I sat back, holding my baby, watching my family, feeling more at peace than I ever had.

***

Spring came again, and I marveled over how much my life had changed in the past year. I was sitting in the same place I was for Liam's first baseball game, but nothing else in my life was the same.

I looked out over the field, catching sight of Jaxon watching us. A chair hadn't been enough for our setup at the edge of the field. Not for Jaxon. He'd put together a little sun tent with cushions and blankets—all in the team colors, of course. There was a cooler and a fan and plenty of toys. We definitely had the best seat in the house. I bounced Lori on my knee, helping her wave her hand at Jaxon. He grinned, blowing us a kiss, then turned to huddle with the team.

The game had been intense so far. They were up against a really tough team for their first game, but Liam had improved tremendously over the past year. No doubt thanks to the wolf strength in him. Jaxon worked religiously with him on his skill and technique. I was pretty sure we had a little All-Star on our hands.

Lori cooed, and I lifted her up and kissed her chubby cheeks. She squealed and giggled, then I brought her in close to nuzzle her.

"Liam's up to bat, Lori. Daddy's telling him what to do." I watched as Jaxon pulled Liam to the side, crouching down next to him and talking to him earnestly. I wished I could hear what they were saying because the fierce determination that crossed Liam's face let me know everyone better watch out. He was on a mission.

"Come on, you can do it," I whispered, Lori wiggling in my arms. I clutched her tightly, holding my breath as Liam strode up to the plate before tapping his bat and positioning himself to swing.

It was the bottom of the ninth, and the bases were fully loaded. Our team had put up a good fight, but we were sitting at three points behind. The fate of the game came down to this moment.

As Liam looked back at Jaxon one last time you could have heard a pin drop in the crowd. Linc stood with Jaxon at the dugout, his eyes darting between Liam, the pitcher, and Cole, who was on first base. Jaxon gave Liam a nod and crossed his arms over his chest, his stance wide as he looked on.

Then Liam turned up to the sky and yelled, "This one's for you, Mom!"

My breath rushed out in a gasp, my chest contracting. I couldn't tear my eyes away. The pitcher took the mound, squared off against Liam. Then he let it fly.

Liam stood, steady and sure, never wavering. At the last possible second, when I was afraid he might not swing, his arms ripped around with a force that sent the ball blurring through the sky.

I jumped to my feet, screaming. The entire crowd was in an uproar. I jumped up and down as the cheers filled the air. Jaxon was at the very edge of the field pointing and shouting. The kids flew around the bases, but there was no rush because Liam had knocked the ball clean out of the park.

I hugged Lori to me, turning to Greer who was sitting on the first bleacher beside me. He was cheering right along. Jaxon was pumping his fist in the air now as the team ran the bases. When Liam's foot crashed down on home plate, the cries grew even louder.

I'd never been caught up in so much excitement. The team ran out, circling Liam, screaming about his grand slam. Then they lifted him high. I waved furiously at him, shouting out my own congratulations. He caught my eye and grinned.

Jaxon ran out on the field next, high fiving the boys and helping Liam to the ground. He wrapped him up in the biggest bear hug. I watched them together, smiling. Greer squeezed my shoulder, and I grinned up at him before looking back at my baby girl.

This was what life was about. Family.

I didn't know how I'd scored such a perfect life, but I wasn't going to question it. I was going to enjoy every second of it. With Jaxon and our family, I'd been the one to knock it out of the park.

Printed in Great Britain
by Amazon